Every Month Original Novels, Stories, and Articles

MONTHLY

USA Today Bestselling Writer
Dean Wesley Smith

TABLE OF CONTENTS

SHORT STORIES

FULL NOVEL

NONFICTION

Smith's Monthly Issue #46

All Contents copyright © 2021 Dean Wesley Smith
Published by WMG Publishing
Cover and interior design copyright © 2021 WMG Publishing
Cover art copyright © by adrenalina /Depositphotos

ISBN-13: 978-1-56146-689-4
ISBN-10: 1-56146-689-1

The Writings and Opinions of
Dean Wesley Smith

Introduction to Issue #46
Time Does Fly...

Issue #44 was dated May 2017. And issue #45 was dated January 2021. Now, here in late January 2021, I am working on the February issue and time keeps on marching on. It struck me that even though there was more than three years between those dates, the feeling was those three years just flashed past. Without a doubt, a lot happened in those three years.

One full year of that was 2020 and we all know how much fun 2020 was. (And still going some here in the early months of 2021 as well, but at least now we have a light at the end of the tunnel, and as I write this it is almost a week since getting my first vaccine.)

For me and Kris, all of 2018 we call the "Year of the Move." I started 2018 with every intention of keeping *Smith's Monthly* going forward, and if I remember, part of the 2018 plan was to catch up on some of the missed months. But by the end of 2017, Kris was getting sick, and in January 2018 I ended up finding us a place to live here in Las Vegas just blocks from two major hospitals.

We moved the next month and Kris got better quickly. But she didn't dare travel, so I spent the rest of the year taking care of WMG Publishing business and getting us out of a massive home on the Oregon Coast that we had settled into over twenty-three years earlier.

And with the back and forth to Oregon, it took me some time to get settled into Las Vegas and all the changes this new life brought. Including to my writing schedule. Took me two of those years to just finally figure out the writing schedule issue and solve it.

Also, in that period we moved the major in-person workshops to Las Vegas and that took a lot of time as well. More than I would have expected, actually.

Besides all that, in the fall of 2017, we decided to bring back *Pulphouse: A Fiction Magazine* and I was the editor. That's right, we did that right before the year of the move, which at that point we did not know was going to be needed.

So, the first eight issues of *Pulphouse* were during 2018 and 2019. When we finally had that under control, I decided I should bring back up this magazine in the spring of 2020. In fact, at one point I had the next issue dated June 2020, so it would just follow exactly after the May 2017 issue.

Well, that didn't happen. 2020.

But now we are through 2020 and the elections here in the States and the vaccines are going out at a faster and faster rate. There seems to be a light in the distance. A perfect moment to bring back this project I love so much.

In essence, for the first time in a while, I have a belief in the future.

For those of you who have been so patient with this crazy project over the years, thank you. I am very proud I got 44 issues done before things got sidetracked, and I am now even prouder to get started again.

Wow, what a wild and crazy three years.

—Dean Wesley Smith
January 25th, 2021

Can't Get Enough of Marble Grant?
These stories and more are available at your favorite booksellers.

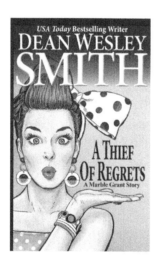

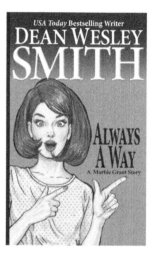

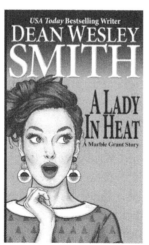

Coming Next Issue in *Smith's Monthly*

RING GAME

A Cold Poker Gang Novel

Smith's

NUMBER FORTY-SEVEN
MARCH, 2021

MONTHLY

*Original Stories,
Novels, and Articles*

DEAN WESLEY SMITH

RING GAME

A Cold Poker Gang Novel

USA TODAY BESTSELLING AUTHOR

DEAN WESLEY SMITH

MYSTERY CAT

A POKER BOY SHORT STORY

Poker Boy often saves the planet, other humans, sometimes other superheroes, and even dogs.

But never a cat, at least until now.

With cats, he needs the help of a superhero of cats, Pahket Jones.

And as typical of Poker Boy, nothing ever remains simple.

Even saving a cat.

Mystery Cat
A Poker Boy Story

ONE

I LOVE LUNCHES in my invisible floating office over the Strip in Las Vegas. You just never knew who was going to show up at noon every day just to enjoy one of Madge's amazing hamburgers and sit and talk.

And in Vegas, it seemed the sun was always shining, so the four glass walls of floor-to-ceiling windows of my office often made it seem like we were actually outside, just sitting in a brightly-lit diner booth floating on a small platform.

I loved my office. Not sure if I ever said that. And it seemed from the different members of the team who stopped by regularly for lunch, everyone did as well, including Lady Luck herself, Laverne, who showed up a couple times a week at least.

On a normal day, as if there ever was such a thing in the superhero universe, the group for lunch included Stan, the God of Poker and my direct boss. Stan never seemed to wear anything but a tan sweater and tan pants and was maybe the blandest and calmest man alive.

Ben, the oldest and smartest of the superheroes, usually showed up as well. He was the only god I had ever met who looked like an old guy, actually an old librarian. The rest of us had just basically stopped aging at thirty. No idea how old Ben actually was, but he was part of the major group that went all the way back more thousands of years than I want to think about.

Patty and I also never seemed to miss a lunch. Patty Ledgerwood, aka Front Desk Girl, was my partner in all things superhero and love and sharing. She was also my best friend and the person who kept me calm and anchored, especially in times when the team had to save the world. We had been a couple for years now and I still had no idea why such a beautiful and powerful woman stayed with me.

Today she was in her MGM Grand uniform and was on her lunch break, her long brown hair pulled back and off her face. It was about ten minutes before noon and she and I were just standing near one wall of my office, talking and watching the cars and tourists below on the Strip. Madge hadn't appeared yet from her diner down off Fremont to see who was around.

There was a doorway from my floating office to a side passage in Madge's diner that allowed those who couldn't teleport to get to my office. And Madge used the door to bring us all food every day.

Suddenly, as we stood there, my warning sense went off that something was wrong. That sense (along with teleporting, slipping between moments of time, and asking stupid questions) was one of my main superpowers.

I glanced around. Nothing in the office, so had to be below.

"Spidey sense just went off," I said to Patty as I turned to study the city below us.

Patty did the same.

For what seemed like an eternity, but had to have been only thirty or so seconds, we studied all the people, cars, and buildings below us. I couldn't see a thing wrong, which is saying something for the Las Vegas Strip. Not even the standard staggering overweight man wearing a bright Hawaiian shirt, shorts, tall white socks, black dress shoes, and carrying a four-foot-high drink.

Nothing.

Finally Patty pointed and said, "There!"

I saw nothing.

"Beside the second palm from the intersection in the middle of the street on the median."

I found the second palm, but still couldn't see what she thought was wrong until a colored orange, brown, and black area near the base of the palm moved and started to dash into the street, right in front of a lot of traffic.

It was a cat with only seconds to live.

"No!" Patty shouted.

I instantly put both of us out of time, stopping the mad dash of the cat and the traffic that was about to end the cat's life.

Then I jumped to the cat in the street. Being in front of frozen cars barreling down on me was not fun. If my stepping between moments of time power slipped, I would end up as a hood ornament.

It was creepy being in the middle of that kind of traffic and there was no sound. None.

And since I hadn't been outside for days, I hadn't realized just how hot it was, especially on that pavement. No wonder the cat was making a run for it.

I grabbed the cat out of mid-stride, tucked it under my arm, and jumped back to the coolness of my office.

"Thank you," Patty said.

Patty wanted to take the cat from me but I shook my head. No way she wanted to be holding a terrified cat when I released us all back into time. And I didn't either, so I sat the cat on the ground, aimed away from the closest glass wall, and released Patty and I back into normal time.

The cat made it almost instantly about halfway across my office before it realized something had changed and stopped, frozen and scared to death.

Then it ran under the booth to hide in the dark right where we were planning to have lunch.

Patty laughed and hugged me. "My hero," she said.

"So now we not only save the world, we save cats and dogs."

"We're going to need some help with this one," Patty said, looking under the booth and talking softly. Then she looked back at me. "Might want to get that superhero of cats you helped a few months back."

"I'll see if she wants to join us for lunch. Be right back."

And with that I jumped to see if I could find Pakhet Jones.

TWO

IT TOOK ME two stops before I found Pakhet Jones. My first stop was to knock on the door at Marble Grant and Sims in the Ogden Condominiums in the downtown area. The only time I had met Pak was there when I helped her rescue a cat from an impossible situation.

Marble, a ghost agent that I could see, appeared in the hallway beside me, looking as stunning as ever in a silk blouse, jeans, and running shoes. She and her partner and love, Sims, would spend their days looking for people to help by crawling inside people's minds.

If I had to wake up every day thinking I would do nothing but be inside other people's minds, I would never get out of bed. But it seems that Marble and Sims and other ghost agents flat loved it. And they helped a lot of people with that power, that was for sure.

Marble told me that Pak had a condo two floors up from hers. And if she wasn't there, try Cabana #7 at the Mandalay Casino pool. It seemed that Pak basically owned that cabana and used it like an office most every day. And that Marble and Sims really enjoyed joining her there at times.

I jumped to outside of Pak's condo and knocked and a moment later the most amazingly beautiful woman answered the door. She saw me and beamed.

"Poker Boy. What a wonderful surprise. Come on in."

With that she turned and led the way back into her white and gold condo with a fantastic view of the entire city of Las Vegas.

Pak was a striking woman in any circumstance, standing over six feet tall and very thin. Her skin was a rich golden color and she was completely bald, with her face and head also a beautiful golden shade.

She had on a black bikini that left little to any imagination and was covered only by a sheer white cover-up that hung open and made the entire look breathtaking.

I know it took my breath away, because it was a ways into her condo before I could say anything.

The black-and-white cat that I had helped her rescue was stretched out in the sun in her living room area and didn't even bother to look up at me.

"I could use your help with a cat," I said.

I told her what had happened and where the cat was a few minutes ago when I left.

"On the Strip?" Pak asked. "There are no homes anywhere near there."

"Some condos a ways south is all," I said.

"So a cat with a mystery," she said, nodding. "Let me slip some clothes over this. I was just about to head to my cabana office."

She vanished through a door as I turned to stare out over the city. Again the cat that I had helped rescue from nearly dying didn't even bother to open an eye and look at me. It even ignored my growling stomach that right now wanted nothing more than a good hamburger and fries and vanilla shake for lunch.

Less than a minute later, Pak came back out wearing a light tan blouse and jeans and running shoes, nearly the same outfit that Marble Grant had been wearing.

"I'll jump us," I said.

And a moment later we were in my office floating over the Strip.

Patty was sitting on the floor in front of the booth clearly trying to comfort the cat. Stan and Ben both stood off to one side looking amused at the entire situation.

I introduced Pak to Patty, then turned to introduce Stan and Ben.

But Pak said, "Ben! Stan! Wonderful to see you both."

Then she hugged them.

I just shook my head. Amazing sometimes how small the god and superhero world was. I would have to ask them later how they knew each other.

Then Pak seemed to realize where she was at and just sort of stopped and looked around, her mouth open.

I smiled. My office tended to do that to people.

Finally she shook her head and looked at the booth. "Is that out of Madge's place down off of Fremont?"

"A replica," I said.

"Might as well be in my place," Madge said, appearing from the invisible door on the other side of the booth. "Good seeing you young woman. You want your normal when this is all finished?"

"I would love that," Pak said, smiling. "Thanks."

Then Pak got down on her hands and knees where Patty had been sitting and looked in under the table.

"So who do we have here?" she said aloud to the cat hunched fearfully as far back in the booth as it could get.

Pak nodded. Then glanced back at me. "His name is Table Stakes, but his human companion just called him Stakes."

That shocked me. That was a poker term, which meant his owner, or companion as cats like to think of the humans they live with, must be a poker player.

"I understand you had an adventure outside," Pak said to the cat. "What were you doing there?"

I knew that Pak could hear the thoughts of cats, but that left the rest of us to try to figure out a one-sided conversation, like she was talking on the phone and we couldn't hear the person on the other end.

Pak nodded after a moment and sat back, turning to look up at the rest of us standing around the room. The look on her face was of anger and worry.

"Stake's companion was drugged and taken by two men from their home. Stake tried to scratch and attack one of the men and was tossed in the trunk of a car with his companion. Stake got out by crawling through the back seat and out a slightly open back window. That was just before you rescued him."

All I could do was stand there and stare.

"Stake believes his companion might be hurt."

At that moment the cat named Stakes, a beautiful and small calico, came out from under the booth and crawled into Pak's lap.

Pak nodded. "We'll do what we can."

Clearly talking to the cat.

THREE

I HAD NO IDEA what to do next. Not one clue. We had a cat who had no idea where he lived, no idea of what color or make a car was, and no way to identify two men who might have hurt a poker player for who knew what reason.

The silence in my office didn't feel normal, that was for sure. Everyone was trying to puzzle this one out.

Finally Pak said to the cat, "How far from where Poker Boy rescued you were you when you escaped the car?"

Pak nodded, then looked up. "Stakes escaped right at the spot you rescued him, but the car he escaped from was going the other way than the ones threatening him."

I nodded. "So the car was going southbound, which means more than likely he came out a back window on the driver's side."

Pak stood and handed Stakes to Patty, who cuddled him and nodded, clearly using her calming powers on the cat to keep it relaxed.

"I got a detective friend," Pak said, "who can get access to cameras that might have seen it. He owes me."

"Superhero?" I asked.

"No," she said, pulling out her phone and hitting a listing. "Just a really nice guy, good cop, nearing retirement."

After a moment she said, "Detective Halligan. It is Pakhet Jones."

She nodded and again we were listening to a one-sided conversation she was having.

"I have a cat problem and I need your help. Are there traffic cams along the Strip?"

She nodded. "Every foot of it? Good, I was hoping for that."

I quickly gave her the address that was right near where the cat escaped.

"A car, going southbound on the Strip, had a cat escape out the back driver's window." She gave him the address, then added, "We really need to find the owner of that car."

"Don't ask," she said after a moment. "Can you just get me the owner of that car's name and address? I'll owe you."

After a moment she said, "Thanks."

She looked around. "Figured it was better at this point to not bring in the possible hurt person until we knew for sure."

I nodded. "Tough to explain."

"It won't take him long," she said, moving over to pet Stakes as Patty held him. Clearly the cat was in heaven at the moment, his paws going in and out.

Less than one minute later her phone played the theme from Hawaii Five-O and she answered it.

"Any luck, Detective?"

She nodded. "Benson Little." And then she repeated the address as if she was writing it down so we all heard it. And then the make of the car. A blue, four-door Buick sedan. Three years old.

But I didn't need all of that. I knew Benson Little from one too many times playing at a poker table with him. The guy was an easy mark, had more tells than a billboard, and just wasn't fun to be around.

And he always had a faint odor of mold and rot on his clothes.

Stan was also shaking his head at the name. He clearly knew Benson as well.

Pak thanked the detective and hung up.

"How bad is this guy, really?" I asked Stan.

"Dangerous," was all that Stan said.

I turned to Patty. "Would you and Ben stay with Stakes?"

Patty nodded.

"Stan, you want to take us to his house out of time?"

Stan nodded and a moment later Stan and I and Pak were standing in the heat of the afternoon in front of the address the detective had given her. It was a single-story run-down home that had seen its last good days in the '80s and been ignored ever since. Pealing paint, nothing but weeds and rocks in the yard. And a closed garage door.

"Inside the garage," I said to Stan and he jumped us there.

Frozen in place were Benson Little and another minor-level poker player who lost more than he won and I had never bothered to remember his name.

They were in the process of lifting professional poker player Jonathan Richard out of the trunk of the car.

Jonathan was a great guy, liked by everyone, and deadly in live high-stakes games. His wife had died a few years ago, and I remember half of the Las Vegas poker community showed up for the funeral.

"Damn it!" Stan said.

"Let's find some wire and whatever to tie these two idiots up," I said.

Pak and I went to what looked like a long unused workbench and found enough zip ties and twine to make sure both men wouldn't move or get away.

The three of us took Jonathan and moved him to a spot on the garage floor, then tied up the other two and put nasty-smelling, oil-covered rags over their eyes and left them sitting on the ground against the dirty car.

"Okay," I said. "Drop us back into time."

Stan released us back into regular time and the sounds of the neighborhood smashed in.

Then Stan and Pak both worked to see if Jonathan was alive.

Thankfully, he was.

"I'll get an ambulance here," Pak said. "After I call Detective Halligan."

"What the hell is going on?" Benson shouted, struggling to get free, but doing nothing but tightening the twine around his wrists and legs. His partner just sat there shaking.

Stan, as calm as any god could be, stood and moved over to Benson, then without even a hesitation or even saying a word, tipped him over and kicked him squarely in the groin.

The sound Benson made was not a sound I ever wanted to hear again. But I laughed and so did Pak. Stan just nodded, calm and collected as you would expect from the God of Poker.

FOUR

THANKFULLY Jonathan awoke just before Detective Halligan got there, so he could explain what Benson and his partner had done and why. Seems they had heard he had a bunch of cash in a safe in his house and they wanted it. They forced him to open the safe and then knocked him out with some sort of drug.

The cash was in a bag with other personal stuff from Jonathan's home on the kitchen table. Jonathan was pretty sure they were going to kill him. Benson had laughed that Jonathan would be just fine in the backyard with the others. So it seemed the police had some digging to do back in the weeds.

Jonathan, right before the ambulance hauled him away, asked me how we had found him. Detective Halligan seemed real interested in that answer as well.

I pointed to Pak. "They tossed Stakes into the trunk with you and he got out and I rescued him and Pak there knew to call Detective Halligan and how to track what needed to be tracked. She is amazing with cats."

"Stakes all right?" Jonathan asked, looking suddenly worried.

"He's in great hands," I said, not lying in the slightest.

So by the time we got back to my office for lunch, it was well after two.

Patty and Ben were sitting in the booth, clearly finished eating, and Stakes was on Patty's lap munching on a fry.

Pak looked at Stake and said, "Your companion is going to be all right. He should be home in a few days. You can stay with me until then."

She nodded and then turned as Madge came in to take our lunch orders.

"What did Stakes say?" I asked.

Pak just laughed as Stakes kept working on the fry.

"He said, 'Good.'"

"That was all he said?" I asked. "I saved his life and we saved his companion's life and all he says is 'Good.'"

"Cats are creatures of few words," Pak said, smiling as she slid into the booth beside Ben.

Patty touched my leg and smiled, "Don't take it personally, just because you aren't."

Ben and Stan both laughed.

I honestly had no idea how to take that.

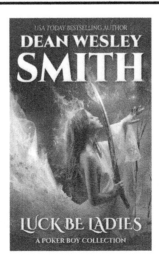

Smith's STORIES

DEAN WESLEY SMITH

USA Today Bestselling Writer

LOST ROBOT

A Sky Tate Short Story

This story resulted from an invitation from Writers of the Future *to write a story around a wonderful Bob Eggleton cover done for Volume 35. One of my first stories appeared in* Writers of the Future Volume #1, *so thirty-five years later, having a story in Volume #35 excited me.*

Plus, I love Bob's art.

So, I wrote this story of a superhero detective from my Poker Boy universe, Sky Tate.

I really love Sky Tate. Expect more stories about her regularly in these pages in coming months.

LOST ROBOT
A Sky Tate Story

ONE

FINDING CLIENTS just never seems to be an issue for me. Not sure if that stems from the vast number of total idiots in the world or my ability to attract those infected by idiocy. Not saying all of my clients are idiots. Most aren't, but most seem to be dealing with stupidity of one sort or another.

In fact, lately, my clients have been wonderful women, attractive women, single women. That has been great fun for me, since I tend to lean toward women far more than men with my sexual life. Luckily, as a detective, there are no written rules about affairs with clients.

Truth of the matter, I was most definitely leaning toward Jean, my new client.

Her full and real name was Jeanette King. No middle name, no initial, nothing. Just Jeannette King. She went by Jean. And first time I saw her walk into Rocky's Bar in the strip mall off Flamingo, I almost melted from the heat, even though the Vegas weather was nice at eighty and Rocky's air-conditioning was working just fine.

Jean had a full head of bright red hair that flared out from her head like a nova and ran down over her shoulders like a lava flow. (So sue me, I get a little descriptive when it comes to Jean, but wow, just wow.)

She had the standard green eyes that went with bright red natural hair and the fair skin covered with a sea of light tan freckles. The freckles went down her neck and vanished under her white silk blouse. My first thought was to want desperately to follow those freckles like a bloodhound following a scent, sniffing and licking all the way.

Jean did that to me right from the start.

I got all that detail through the wave of lust sweeping over me, and she hadn't even started across the small bar yet. Being a superhero detective and super observant at everything had its advantages and disadvantages at times.

Jean had on jeans (go figure), running shoes, and a smile that seemed to light up her red hair even more as she came toward me across the small dance floor off the bar.

She had been referred to me by a friend at the main police station and I knew instantly I was going to have to send him a bottle of fine whiskey for the referral, no matter what her case turned out to be.

I had been sitting at the bar, working on a Diet Coke, waiting for her, when she came in. She reached me and my open mouth and staring eyes and stuck out her hand.

"You must be Sky Tate," she said.

"I am," I said, managing to get my hand into her fine-skinned grip.

"Oh, you're a woman," Jean said.

Then she blushed.

I loved the blush. It lit up the trail of her freckles.

"I noticed that too when I took a shower this morning," I said.

She blushed even more.

The bar got warmer.

Lots of people thought I was a guy because I had a habit of wearing the standard detective gray trench coat and a gray fedora. The hat tended to hide my longer hair because I kept it tied up and covered when working, and the trench coat covered what assets I did have without any issue at all.

Plus my face was long and I had what many call a Roman nose. I call it a beak.

So with all that, being mistaken for a guy with the name Sky Tate wasn't anything new. And I often used that to my advantage in cases.

"I'm sorry," Jean said.

"Don't be," I said, taking off my hat and coat and letting my hair fall down over my shoulders. "I tend to hide some. A detective thing."

She nodded to that. Amazing how using the detective-thing excuse allowed me to get away with a lot.

I motioned that we should move to a small table off to one side so we could talk in private, even though Rocky was the only other person in the place and most of the time he was hard of hearing. One reason I liked the place.

One of my superpowers was being able to completely read a person's problems by simply shaking their hand. When I shook Jean's hand, not only did I get a little tingling (that had nothing to do with the case), but I saw her problem and why she wanted to hire me.

Her father, Carl, was dying. Nasty cancer. He didn't have long, that much was clear.

Now I might be a superhero, but I sure didn't have the power to keep anyone alive or bring them back from the dead. But her problem was that her father, who seemed to be clear in the head with all other matters, had started telling her this wild story that back in the 1960s, when he was just out of college and before he headed to Vietnam, he had found a gigantic sentient robot up by Lake Mead.

And for a time, he and the robot had become friends. From what her father had said, the robot could read his thoughts, kind of like I was reading Jean's thoughts when I touched her hand. It seems that the robot had gotten separated from the others of his kind and was hiding. It had sworn his father to secrecy.

Then her father had been drafted into the war in Vietnam and by the time he had returned, the robot had vanished. Her father had told no one, not even his wife, until he finally told his daughter as he was dying.

Now I am sure that any normal detective, or anyone for that matter, would have laughed, but I was no normal detective, and over the two hundred years of my life, I had seen a lot of really strange stuff. Granted, no giant robots, but damned near everything else.

"First off," I said to Jean, "I am sorry about your father's illness."

She looked startled.

"Another detective thing," I said, smiling at her. "So you want to tell me what I can do to help?"

She nodded, took a deep breath, and then basically told me the story I already knew about her father and his tale of a giant robot in Lake Mead.

I nodded all the way through the story, not saying a thing.

Finally Jean said, "You're not laughing."

I wanted to say that I would never laugh at a woman as good-looking as she was, but instead said, "I take all my client's stories seriously."

"Thank you," she said, blushing slightly again. "All I really want is to let my father know I am taking him seriously and looking for his lost robot."

She looked like she might burst into tears at that moment, but managed to hold it together. I could only imagine the courage this was taking for her to tell anyone such a wild story.

"I understand," I said, wanting to reach out and touch her hand, but resisting, a feat, I might add, that was difficult.

She nodded and I gave her a moment to compose herself. Besides, I loved just staring at her. Not very professional for a detective like me, I must admit, but I didn't often face someone as beautiful as Jean.

"I would like to meet your father," I said to her after a long moment. "Would that be possible?"

"So you will help me?"

"I will do my best, and nothing less," I said. "We will make sure your father knows we believe him and are doing our best for him in his final days."

Now tears really did reach her eyes and she smiled.

"How much is your fee?"

"Let's not worry about that," I said. "Can I meet your father now?"

She nodded. And gave me directions to his house, which I already knew, of course.

"I will follow you," I said. "I have a white Cadillac that I can do a little research in and get my assistants to help while we drive."

I didn't have any assistants, but I figured I would set that up in case I learned something from her father I needed to cover.

Again she smiled and stood. "You have no idea how much I appreciate this."

"Let's see what we can do," I said.

I had little hope at all that we could do much more than help a dying man get some peace, but watching Jean walk from that bar ahead of me was worth far more than I wanted to admit.

TWO

JEAN'S father's house sat in one of those desert subdivisions that looked all the same. All were gated with winding streets and evenly-spaced palm trees. Only slight differences in the desert landscaping of each brown-toned house and the large address numbers on the front by the two-car garages allowed anyone to tell them apart. I hated subdivisions like this one, no matter how well-kept they looked. They felt more like warehouses for humans than actual distinctive places to live. That's why I lived in the Ogden Condos that were square in the middle of the downtown area. It was a beautiful high-rise condo that looked out over the constant party that was Fremont Street.

Jean waited for me to park on the street, her massive red hair glowing in the afternoon sun like a goddess. I had met my share of real goddesses over the two centuries, including Lady Luck herself, but none of them could hold a candle to Jean's beauty.

Or maybe I was just being really conflicted by the lust at the moment. That was more than likely the case.

We went through the open garage and into the kitchen area of the modern home. It was clean, as I would have expected, with no dishes in the sink or on the counter.

The morning paper, actual old-style print newspaper, took up part of the kitchen table, and the sounds of a football game came from another room. Everything was in brown tones, including the kitchen tile and eggshell paint on the walls.

The living room was more brown, with expensive furniture and only splashes of color from a pillow or a flower in a vase.

I knew Jean's father lived here alone since her mother had died five years before. And I knew he was well-off when it came to money. Clearly someone did the cleaning for him as well.

As we entered the living room, Jean said, "Daddy, I have company. Someone to meet you."

The man with the balding head in the chair glanced back, then clicked off the television and stood without issue. Clearly he was in good shape except for the cancer that was about to kill him.

"This is Detective Sky Tate," Jean said. "Detective Tate, this is my father Carl King."

Carl laughed. "You hired a detective?"

Jean just smiled at him fondly. "I wanted to see what we could find out."

I had left my trench coat and fedora in the car and still had my hair down, so I looked fairly normal.

"Nice to meet you, Detective," Jean's father said, reaching forward to shake my hand.

And the moment I touched his dry skin and firm grip, I knew for a fact he was telling Jean the truth about finding a giant robot in Lake Mead.

He really had.

I flat didn't know what to think about that.

The robot had a pointed head, two rocket-looking packs on its back, two arms, two legs, and no mouth. Its eyes were black as night and Carl had communicated with it through thoughts.

The robot had clearly been hiding for some time, mostly underwater, when Carl came into contact with it in a cave in the rocks in an area of Lake Mead that was now, all these years later, above the water line, since the lake level had gone down so far.

I held onto his hand a moment too long, then finally let go. The shock that over fifty years ago there was a giant robot in Lake Mead took me a moment to adjust to, I had to admit.

"I am sure sorry to hear about your illness, sir," I said.

He shrugged. "I survived Nam, figured something was going to take me out eventually."

I smiled at him and then at Jean.

Jean got us all some water and we sat at the kitchen table, with Jean between me and her dad.

Then I leaned forward and looked him directly in the eye, making sure he understood I was listening as intently as anyone had ever listened to him. That was one of my main superpowers, besides reading thoughts and the ability to teleport.

Then I said simply, "Tell me about this robot you found."

And he did, detail for detail, awkward at times because he clearly hadn't told this story much at all. He started by detailing the times of the 1960s, about how he had gone up to Lake Mead to get away from the knowledge that he was going to be drafted. He had been trying to decide whether to go into the service or flee to Canada. He had already run through his student deferment.

He had been using a small rented rowboat that day and found the cave in the rocks late in the afternoon, hidden from view of the main traffic on the lake. The robot had been underwater and when he rowed into the cave, it appeared.

Turns out it was lonely. After the shock at being able to understand what a giant robot was saying, Carl said he had relaxed and it seemed the two of them had similar issues. Carl felt lost and the robot was lost, separated from the other robots in his group.

The robot had been hiding there since right after the dam had filled.

Over the next few weeks, Carl went back every day and, by talking to the robot, Carl came to realize he needed to face his future and not hide from it. So he told the robot he hoped to survive the war and return. He said that knowing that robot was there kept him alive in Vietnam more than anything.

But when he got back, the robot was gone. Once or twice a year, Carl went back to the same area, searching for it, but could not find any sign of it.

"My only hope," Carl said finally, "was that the robot found his own kind."

I nodded.

It had been clear from Carl's thoughts that the existence of that robot had got him through the war and kept him going through hard times in his life.

"Can you show me on a map exactly where this cave is?"

He frowned, clearly feeling slightly shocked that someone was giving his story complete credence, and then stood and headed off down the hallway to a back room.

Jean reached over and touched my arm, a smile on her face and tears in her eyes. "Thank you."

I flat loved her touch, but strangely enough, at the moment, my entire interest had turned to finding that robot. I really believed that it had existed, as Carl said, and the superhero detective in me really wanted to find it.

Carl came back with a map and easily showed me exactly the rock wall where the cave was. I asked if I could take the map and he agreed.

"I got some friends who might be able to help me with this," I said, standing and refolding the map. "We will see what we can find."

He shook my hand again and I could read how pleased he was that I was taking him seriously. He had no expectations, but clearly I had done what Jean wanted me to do in his last days.

Jean walked me out to my car and once again shook my hand. I could feel her interest in me at that point, and before I'd heard Carl's story, that would have melted me right there in the afternoon sun. It still did my heart good, and I looked forward to what might be a wonderful time after I solved this case.

But right now the time wasn't right for either of us. I had a lost robot to find, or at least prove it had existed at one point in time. No small case. But I loved the challenge.

And I didn't get that many really challenging cases after two hundred years on the job.

So lust was just going to have to wait.

THREE

EVERY ASPECT of life has gods and superheroes attached. I am a superhero in the detective area. We live a long time, possibly forever, and we have special powers that help us in our profession.

There are food gods, sports gods of every type, and even poker gods and superheroes. One of the most famous is Poker Boy. His girlfriend is a superhero in the hotel hospitality area and Poker Boy calls her Front Desk Girl, but not to her face.

What I needed for help was a superhero in the area of lost-and-found items. And in the Las Vegas area, I only knew of one.

Plane.

I mean, I at least had a second name that went with Sky, but Plane, as far as I knew, only went by one. Just Plane, the kind that flies, not the boring kind. That was his standard line.

Plane topped the scales at well over four hundred pounds and lived in a giant home just outside of Vegas that had to be the size of a major grocery store, filled to the ceiling in most places with stuff.

He always wore silk suits and bright ties that he never tied completely. He wore standard, white tennis shoes with his silk suits and kept a baseball cap on his head at all times.

On top of that, Plane was a hoarder. He would be a cliché if he wasn't older than I was and as rich as most countries from buying and selling stuff.

He was one of those hoarders who knew exactly where everything was in every pile and the current value of it on the open market. I had only been in his home once, about five years before, but he took a liking to my beak of a nose. Not sure why, maybe it was so strange it was collectable.

So I parked my caddy in my spot in the Ogden parking garage, and teleported out to his place. I had warned him I had something really special that needed finding and he had just grunted and said, "Get here before dinner."

Since it was only just before noon, I figured I had some time.

I found him sitting in his big office chair surrounded by at least a dozen computer screens, all showing auctions going around the world.

He put his finger up for me to be silent and wait and less than one minute later he sighed and turned to face me. From what I could tell he had lost all the auctions he had been bidding on. I said nothing. Last thing I wanted was to get a collector going on the unfairness of the new world of computers and eBay and the internet.

"So what are you looking for?"

"A giant robot. Real, telepathic, about sixty feet or so tall, vanished in the Lake Mead area in the 1960s."

He stared at me for a moment with tiny, dark eyes that I wasn't certain could see out of the rolls of fat on his forehead and cheeks, then said, "You aren't kidding, are you?"

I shook my head. "Client's father made friends with it back in the 1960s before he shipped off to Vietnam. The robot was gone when he got back and now the guy is dying of cancer and wanted to tell his story."

Plane knew my powers, knew I had read the guy's mind to see if he was telling the truth. So he just nodded.

I pulled out the folded map and put it on a pile of papers near Plane so he could see it, then pointed at the spot. "A cave that was at the water line back then. He says he goes back out there twice a year to see if the robot has returned."

Plane nodded and stood. "You want to jump us there or you want me to."

"Safer if you do it," I said. I didn't feel good about trying to land someone of his bulk on a pile of rocks.

He nodded and a moment later we were standing on rocks about a hundred feet above the waterline of the lake. There was a dry wind blowing and I felt damned happy the temperatures were moderate today. On a hot summer day, this would be an oven.

Plane was looking behind us and after a moment pointed and said, "There."

He jumped us into the mouth of a cave that clearly had been under water at one point.

"This is the place I saw in his mind," I said, nodding.

Plane again jumped us to a spot above the waterline in the back of the cave, then said simply, "Brace yourself, this rewinding time thing can get a little crazy-making."

With that, outside the cave the sun started blinking like a strobe light as Plane took us back in time until eventually in front of us the cavern filled with water.

Then he slowed it down and I caught a glimpse of a young man in a rowboat.

"Here," I said.

Plane had already stopped time.

"No worry, he can't see us," Plane said. "We're outside the time stream."

I nodded, thankful he had answered my unasked question.

As we watched, a young guy, clearly the Carl I had met before he went off to war, rowed slowly into the cave.

And as he got to the back edge, just as I'd seen in his mind, a pointed-headed robot came up out of the water slowly. I found it very impressive that Carl didn't instantly panic and row like hell out into the lake, but eventually it became clear they were talking.

After Carl left that day, the robot simply sank back into the water.

Plane sped us forward to the next day and then the next until finally it was clear that Carl was saying goodbye. This time the robot watched him row away before he sank back into the water.

Three months later, we watched the robot wade out of the now-shallow cave and into deep water.

"Okay," Plane said, "I got the robot's signature. If it is still on the planet, I'll find it."

Plane flashed us back to the present. Then seemed to focus far away.

I waited as patiently as I could until he returned to his beady eyes. "He's still here, along with a couple dozen friends."

"What?" I asked, stunned.

Plane pointed to the deepest part of the lake in front of us "They are living down there. And I got a hunch this is bigger than both of us."

I nodded and looked slightly upward. "Laverne. I think Plane and I have found a problem. Would you join us for a moment?"

In all my years that was only the third time I had called Laverne, Lady Luck herself. She ran everything and was the most powerful god there was.

She appeared beside me dressed in a dark silk power suit that fit her thin body perfectly. She had her long dark hair pulled back tight, which gave her thin face a stern look.

She flat scared the hell out of me. The most powerful being in all the universe would do that to a normal person.

"Yes," she said.

I did a very quick summary of my client, her father, and what Plane and I had just seen in the 1960s.

"Pointed heads, jet packs on the back, dark eyes?" Lady Luck asked.

Plane and I both nodded.

"Maybe thirty of them down there," Plane said.

"Well, shit," Lady Luck said. "That's where they went."

"You knew about them?" I asked, trying to keep my voice level.

She nodded, staring down into the lake below us. "Back when we fought the Titans, before Atlantis, we created them to help us and a world for them to live on. Most were destroyed in the battles, but they helped turn the tide. After the war and then with Atlantis going down, we lost track of the survivors because without our help they couldn't go home. And honestly I had never thought of them for centuries until now. We called them Lightning."

"That's why the lightning bolts painted on them?"

She nodded. "Amazing they are still here and hiding after all these years. We need to get them out of there and get them home. More than likely they have no idea the war is even over."

"The war with the Titans?" Plane asked.

Laverne nodded.

My knowledge of the history of the gods and superheroes was slim, at best. I just couldn't imagine how long ago that war was, or how old Lady Luck really was.

"Where is their home?" I asked.

"Deep in space," she said, waving her hand and dismissing my question. "I'm going to need help with this. I want to thank you both for this incredible find. We owe it to the Lightning to get them home."

"I have one favor to ask," I said before she could vanish. And I asked and she laughed and said, "Of course."

So three days later Jean and I were in a rented speedboat that had towed Carl in a small rowboat out to the area where I knew the robots were. I hadn't told Jean or her father a thing, just that I had a surprise for them. Both of them thought I was being stupid, but they went along.

The evening was still warm and thankfully the wind was fairly calm, so the waves on the lake weren't bad at all. I normally wasn't a fan of small boats, but for this, I wasn't going to miss it, even if I had to dogpaddle out here.

After we unhooked Carl's boat from the speedboat, I turned off the engine and pointed to a spot. We watched him row toward it. For a man near death, he was surprisingly strong.

As he reached the spot, a metal pointed head slowly eased up out of the water.

We all just watched as the robot got about halfway out of the water and stopped, facing Carl directly.

Clearly the two of them were having a conversation, but from our distance, we couldn't hear Carl's side of it, even though he was speaking aloud.

Finally Carl nodded and the robot moved a little farther away and then silently its rocket packs fired and it lifted out of the water and into the air and was gone into the late afternoon blue sky.

I started the speedboat and we went over to where Carl just sat in the rowboat, head down, smiling. We got him back into the speedboat and the rowboat tied to the stern.

"Are you all right, Dad?" Jean said, putting a jacket over Carl's shoulder.

Carl smiled and nodded. "He's just like me. He's a survivor, and he finally gets to go home after his war. And now, so do I."

Then Carl just sat there smiling in the back of the boat and there just wasn't a thing Jean or I could say.

Five weeks later I got a call from Jean that her father had passed away in his sleep, peacefully. I attended the funeral two days later.

Two weeks after that Jean called me to talk. I figured she wanted to know how I had done what I had managed to do for her father. And that was going to be a tough topic to get through.

But it didn't turn out that way.

The two of us sat with glasses of wine and then had a great dinner. And besides getting to know a little more about each other, we talked mostly about her father and his incredible life, how he had finally gotten to come home from his war.

And how he had helped his friend do the same.

~

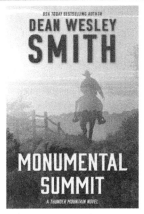
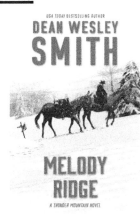

USA TODAY BESTSELLING AUTHOR

DEAN WESLEY SMITH

HOW TO WRITE A NOVEL IN TEN DAYS

A WMG WRITER'S GUIDE

Even in today's fast-paced world, the myth that writing fast equals writing badly—or, conversely, writing well equals writing slowly—persists. Now, USA Today bestselling author Dean Wesley Smith aims to shatter this myth once and for all with this latest WMG Writer's Guide.

In a series of blog posts, Smith chronicled his process toward ghost writing a 70,000-word novel for a traditional publisher in just ten days. He wrote about his progress, his feelings about the writing, and how he approached and overcame obstacles. This book takes readers on a journey that demonstrates that writing fast, and writing well, comes from motivation and practice.

How to Write a Novel in Ten Days
A WMG Writers' Guide

INTRODUCTION

THIS BOOK IS PRETTY EASY TO EXPLAIN. It is simply a series of twelve blog posts, one per day, that I did over a stretch of 12 days just under a year ago. The point of the blogs was to detail out a novel I wrote for a traditional publisher in ten days. I had one post ahead of the writing days and one after I finished the book to wrap up.

All twelve are here.

Now granted, as each day went on, I added to the post, and at the end of the day I did a summary on each post. So if you were following this (as thousands were on my web site hour-by-hour), you would see each post grow as each day went on.

The goal of doing the blogs was to help take out the mystery of "writing" fast and show how it can be done easily. You just spend the time. Writing fast is not typing fast, it's just sitting in the chair and writing for numbers of hours.

A little background: I have written and sold over a hundred novels to traditional publishers over the last twenty-five years. Some years I wrote a great deal, some years I took off during those twenty-five years and wrote no books. But after a hundred plus novels, I know how to write a novel.

I wrote this into the dark, as some writers call this type of writing. In other words, I had no outline. And the novel was published by the publisher with no rewrites from me.

I have left all the blog posts pretty much as I wrote them here in this book, because I felt that would be the best way to detail out the feeling of those ten days.

So I hope this journey through the daily writing process of a novel by a professional novelist is fun and entertaining and enlightening.

I had fun detailing out the process as well.

Enjoy the journey and have fun with your own writing.

—Dean Wesley Smith
February 10th, 2014
Lincoln City, Oregon

A BLOG POST ABOUT THE NOVEL...

As I have said a few times over the last six months, I was hired to write a ghost novel for a major author. I will never tell anyone who the author is or even why I am writing this for this author. Not a word. Ever, so don't ask. But I can tell you that when this comes out of New York, it will be a major bestseller because this author's books always are.

I have been paid the advance, so I plan on starting the novel next week as soon as this great workshop that is going on here at the coast is finished. Character Voice and Setting workshop. Wonderful fun. Great writers.

I will blog here about the writing process of the book, more than likely putting up five or six posts per day about each session and a post at the end of the day summing it all up.

I hope to write the book (70,000 words) in 7 to 10 days and then turn it in to the publisher. One draft.

So if you want to follow the writing process of a novel like this, learn how to write a novel in a short period of time, check back regularly. I'll also tell you about the other things going on in my day as it goes along.

And I will talk about my moods, my feelings, and so on about the writing.

I do not have an outline and will be just writing off into the dark on this one, so it might get kind of scary and entertaining. I hope, anyway, because I hate being bored when I write. (grin)

And I'll be glad to answer questions as it goes along about the writing process. (Not about the book itself in any fashion.)

See you soon. It will be fun for me. I hope it will entertain others in the actual writing process.

DAY ONE

As I said in the previous post, I'm going to have posts here for the ghost novel writing process. (And no, this is not a novel about ghosts, this is me ghosting a novel because I was hired by a publisher.)

I will add to this post at different times today right up until I head to bed so you can follow the process. At the end of each post I will add up the daily word count and project word count. You want to see what a professional writer's day is like, I'll put it up here, every day until this book is done.

Here we go…this might be interesting in a perverse sort of way.

DAY 1, ENTRY 1:

12:45 PM: Rolled out of bed because my big, fluffy white cat—Walter White Kitty …not my fault or his fault for that name…blame Kris (my wife, Kristine Kathryn Rusch)—decided I needed to be up and awake. (I went to bed about 5 am after watching far too much about the tragic events in Boston.)

1:15 PM: I got to my Internet computer with my breakfast bars and did e-mail and answered questions and such. It was luckily an easy morning.

1:45 PM: Moved to my writing computer, set up files, set up a chapter template since I keep a different file for every chapter and combine them at the end, then typed in a title, typed in the main character's name and started writing. I have no idea where this book is going, but to start I paid attention to making up some setting through the character's eyes and opinions.

2:20 PM: About 500 words done. Headed off to get the snail mail and then a meeting at WMG Publishing. At 3:15 met Kris for lunch since she had also been out and running around doing errands. Then back to WMG Publishing and then back here to my home office.

4:15 PM: checked my e-mail, had copyedits sent to me from an editor on a short story. He promised they were light, so I spent thirty minutes doing that and getting the story back to the editor. I then did other e-mail and workshop questions as well and did this first part of this post.

5:05 PM: headed back to my writing computer.

DAY 1, ENTRY 2:

5:05 PM: Moved over to my writing computer from my Internet computer and decided that before I went too far I needed to start a glossary of terms, character dress, place names and such, so I set that up and put in it the little bits I had done in the first 500 words.

Then wrote about 700 words until about 6 PM, took a five minute break, came back and wrote another 500 words before my cat, Walter (Or as Kris now calls him at times The Waltise Falcon) reminded me in no uncertain terms that it was time for a nap.

6:30 PM: checked my e-mail, answered one, grabbed the cat and headed for the downstairs media room to take a nap with the cat. Kris woke me at 7 and we watched news and ate dinner. I did the dishes, tossed in a load of laundry, and headed back for my office. I answered more e-mails, started one more thing for another editor that needs to be done this weekend, then wrote this second entry.

Time is now 8:15 PM and I am headed back to the writing computer. Total so far today around 1,700 words on the book. I'm feeling pretty good about the start so far.

DAY 1, ENTRY 3:

9:30 PM: (This is put up slightly late since the Internet connection was down until after four in the morning, but this is what I would have said.)

I did about 1,300 words between 8:15 and 9:45. Then a fire alarm here in the house went off without reason. Something silly like a dying battery. So by the time I fixed that, Kris offered me a snack so I had a snack with her, then headed back up to the WMG offices to work on some collectable books there as a break.

I got back around 11:00 and tried to put this entry up, but couldn't because of the Internet connection being down, so went to work. At that point I was at around 3,000 words and feeling really fine for the first day.

DAY 1, ENTRY 4:

From 11:00 PM until around midnight I did another session, another 800 words, then took a break and went downstairs to our media room and watched the news and part of Craig Ferguson with Kris.

12:45 AM: went back to work, did about another 1,000 words in just over an hour, took another break and again tried to get online. Kris was headed to bed, so she let me use her iPad to put up a comment to tell everyone what was happening, which was all it was allowing me to do.

2:00 AM: went back to the writing computer, got about another 1,000 words done in another hour. Took a short break, Internet connection still down. Went back to work.

3:00 AM: Internet connection still down, I did about another 1,000 words,

but turned on my e-mail so that it would make a sound when an outgoing message finally got out.

4:10 AM: I did about another 1,000 words before my Internet computer dinged and told me the Internet was back up and working. So I stopped and came to this computer to do this post.

At this point at 4:26 in the morning, I'm at 7,625 words for the day. I could go a little farther but this is a ton better than I had hoped for the first day so I'm going to stop and go downstairs with my cat and veg out on some stupid television.

I still have no idea at all where this book is going. Just making it up as I go. But at the same time I'm feeling no worry at the moment either. I have a hunch that will come.

TOTAL:
Day #1—7,625 words

Feeling great, happy with the first day. Best first day on a novel I've had in some time, to be honest.

Back tomorrow for Day Two. (Remember, my day starts when I drag my butt out of bed, which considering I'll be watching television for the next hour to clear the damn book from my mind so I can sleep, getting out of bed will be around 1 PM.)

DAY TWO

As I said in the previous post, I'm going to have one post per day here for the "ghost" novel writing process that I was hired by a New York publisher to do. I am aiming for 7 to 10 days to finish this novel. I can give ZERO hints about the content of the book, so please don't ask. I am only talking about the writing process and my day around the writing process.

I will add to this post at different times during the day right up until I head to bed so you can follow the process. At the end of each post I will add up the daily word count and project word count. You want to see what a professional writer's day is like, I'll put a post up here every day until this book is done.

I would start reading from Day One and read the comments under that day as well for a ton of answers to questions.

Day One total word count was 7,625 words. So now on to Day Two.

DAY 2, ENTRY 1:

1:15 PM: Rolled out of bed and by 1:45 PM I had my breakfast bars and was answering my e-mail and comments on Day 1 of this. Some good questions. Make sure if you are following this to read the comments and my answers on each day.

2:40 PM now…About one hour of email and comments. About normal for me. Now off to do the first session or two. Back later with another entry in this day.

DAY 2, ENTRY 2:

3:30 PM: I got about 700 words done in the first session, then Kris and I headed off to get the mail and have a quick lunch. Kris is in the last third of a new Kris Nelscott Smokey Dalton novel, so this house is great fun at the moment, since I'm living in this book and she's living in 1970 Chicago.

4:40 PM: Back from lunch and back to work. Got about 1,000 more words

done before needing to take a break at 5:50 PM. The ocean outside my window is flat and it's a beautiful day here on the Oregon Coast. The sun is reflecting off the ocean and making this office heat up even though I have the window wide open, which the cats love. But that makes it hard to type at times, let me tell you. [I know, tiny violin. (grin)]

I answered some e-mail and then some comments. It's now 6:15 PM and I'm headed back to my writing computer for another session before naps with Walter White Kitty (Or as Kris is now calling him, the Waltese Falcon) before dinner.

Total original word count so far today 1,718 words.

DAY 2, ENTRY 3:

7:05 PM: I managed to get almost another thousand words from 6:15 PM. Then I took a break, grabbed the big fluffy white guy and headed for the basement for a nap. Kris woke me and the cat at 7:30 and we ate in front of the news. I did the dishes and headed back to my office.

8:30 PM: Answered e-mails and a number of questions in the comments. And wrote this far in this entry. It's now 8:55 and with a cup of tea in hand I'm headed back to my writing computer. Window over the ocean still open and the ocean air smells wonderful tonight.

Total so far today around 2,700 words.

DAY 2, ENTRY 4:

9:50 PM: I managed another 700 words. Slower than the other sessions because a new viewpoint character decided he/she needed to talk. Sigh. Had to create the character and that's just slower to start.

Then after 700 words I decided I needed a break and headed up to the WMG Publishing offices to work on sorting some collectables and organizing some stuff up there. I got back here about 10:50 and made myself another cup of tea and got a snack and am heading to the writing computer again.

So by 11:00 PM the day has managed around 3,400 words. About on pace. I'm feeling fine as well, not in the slightest bit tired. So far this has not been a strain in the slightest. Tomorrow may be another matter.

DAY 2, ENTRY 5:

12:10 AM: I managed yet another thousand words or so from 11:00 PM. Ran right into a tough scene, stopped cold. So I went downstairs and watched a show with Kris in the media room. Now I feel like going at it again.

It's 1:20 AM and I'm headed back to the writing computer. Back later for one final Day 2 update and the totals so far at that point.

DAY 2, ENTRY 6:

2:10 AM: I finished another 1,000 or so words from 1:20 until 2:10, then took a break. Got back to the writing computer at 2:30 AM.

3:50 AM. I wrote pretty much straight through from 2:30 with only a minor break to move around. Then I flat ran out of gas. Brain said, "Go to bed." But I didn't type that. (grin)

Me and the white cat are headed downstairs to veg on television for a short time before heading to bed.

My daily word count is 7,734 words for Day Two.

TOTALS:
Day #1—7,625 words
Day #2—7,734 words
Total so far—15,359 words.

On pace and on target, which surprises me, to be honest. I am always slower up front, so if I follow pattern I will pick up more words by Thursday or Friday and maybe even finish it Friday or Saturday. We shall see. Lots of slips between here and there. (grin)

See you all for Day Three.

DAY THREE

DAY 3, ENTRY 1:

12:45 PM: Rolled out of bed and by 1:15 PM I had my breakfast bars and was answering my e-mail and comments on Day 2 of this. Some good questions. Make sure if you are following this to read the comments and my answers on each day.

I finished most of the questions and my e-mail just before 2:00 PM and then Kris and I headed off to the normal Sunday writer lunch. Eight other professional fiction writers there today besides us. Great conversation.

Got back here around 4:00 PM, answered more questions and some more e-mail and did this post, and am now, at 4:20 PM heading over to my writing computer for my first session.

DAY 3, ENTRY 2:

4:20 PM: I worked for about an hour, took a five minute break. Ended up with pretty close to 1,000 words in that hour. That seems to be about the pace this book is flowing at. I sometimes only go around 800 words per hour with my four-finger typing, but this one, in most places, is flowing nicely.

5:30 PM: went back for a second session and finished another thousand words. It's now 6:32 and I'm headed to the media room to take a nap with good old Walter White Kitty. (And yes, at some point I'll put a picture of the guy here during this week.)

Total so far on Day 3...Around 2,000 words.

DAY 3, ENTRY 3:

Walter and I napped until 7:00 PM. Then we had dinner and I got back to my office around 7:30 PM.

10:00 PM: I haven't done another word on the novel yet tonight. From 7:30 until about ten minutes ago I was working on the Cliffhangers workshop. For those of you who don't know, I teach some online workshops and each of the writers in the online workshop turn in an assignment each week if they want. So I write them each a letter talking about their assignment, then do a video that talks about the assignment in general and I put it up with the following week's videos.

If you want any information about the online workshops, the descriptions and how to sign up are up under the Online Workshops tab.

10:10 PM: headed back to my writing computer finally. I still have some workshop stuff to do later in the evening, but I can do that on breaks.

DAY 3, ENTRY 4:

10:10 PM: I headed back to my writing computer and managed to get about 1,000 more words done by 11:00 PM.

I took a break, read the March 15th issue of *Publisher's Weekly*, had a snack, and went back to work at about 11:15 PM: I managed yet another 1,000 words and then came to do this entry. Right now it's just after midnight and I'm going to go get a snack and get back to it.

Total so far today around 4,000 words.

DAY 3, ENTRY 5:

1:00 AM: I made it back to the writing computer just after midnight and in fifty minutes managed about another 1,000 words. That sure seems to be my output for a session on this book. That's great. I always like books that do this, much more than the books that won't let me do more than 800 words a session.

Then I took a break and worked on some more workshop stuff, this one for a coast workshop. The difference between the coast workshops here we do five or so times per year and the online workshops is that the coast workshops are like graduate level workshops, while the online workshops are for all levels. The coast workshops are invite only as well. Then went back to the computer and got another few hundred words done before hitting a point I felt stuck.

1:30 AM: So now to a break and then back to write the next sentence. I don't think this is a major stuck, more of a type of stuck that I just got ahead of the back of my brain is all. Ten minutes and I'll be back at it.

Still not a clue at all where this book is going. Not one. But I am liking the characters I came up with, so that's helping. Now if I just don't have to kill one of them along the way. (grin)

DAY 3, ENTRY 6:

1:45 AM: Fired on, clearly not stuck at all like I thought. I just needed a break so my fingers stopped and pretended I was stuck. They do that when I try to continue on too long in one session. (grin)

I got another 1,000 or so words done by 2:30 AM before taking a short break and working on the workshop stuff I had to do.

2:45 AM: back at the fiction computer, got another 1,000 or so words done. It's now 3:40 and I'm out of steam. I have done more work on the workshop as well and might spend a few more minutes on that before heading to bed.

TOTALS:
Day #1—7,625 words
Day #2—7,734 words
Day #3—7,059 words
Total so far—22,418 words

This still feels like a 7 or 8 day pace. We shall see how the next few days go and if it picks up speed some. If not, I'm looking at 9 days. But I'm pretty happy with this start so far.

DAY FOUR

DAY 4, ENTRY 1:

12:45 PM: Rolled out of bed this morning at the same time as yesterday, even though I had ended up watching a stand-up comic last night until 5:30 in the morning. Ah, well. By 1:15 PM I had my breakfast bars and was answering my e-mail and comments on Day 3 of this. Some good questions. Make sure if you are following this to read the comments and my answers on each day.

2:15 PM: I finished the comments and questions and basic e-mail. And finished getting up the online workshop response for the Cliffhangers Workshop I should have finished last night but spaced it. Now I'm heading out to get the mail and head up to WMG Publishing to see what's happening up there. (I'll cause my normal hour of disruption at WMG and then head back here, grabbing some lunch on the way.)

DAY 4, ENTRY 2:

5:00 PM: Not one new fiction word yet written, but headed to the writing computer shortly. I spent time at the post office, then one bank, then up to WMG where I helped them deal with setting up a web site that will hold a novel of Kris's that WMG is going to be serializing starting tomorrow. Check out www. WMGPublishing.com for that. It's a brand new novel called "Spree." A wonderful mystery.

Then I went to yet another bank, then grabbed some lunch at Subway and came home and ate it with Kris while she ate her lunch as well. Then back to this computer to answer more e-mails and do more workshop stuff, and now doing this entry. So now, just a minute or so before 5 PM I'm headed for my writing computer for the first time today.

It's a beautiful day on the Oregon Coast, but the ocean outside my window is a little rough from a north wind. And it's scary bright in here, especially for a person used to working at night. (grin)

DAY 4, ENTRY 3:

7:00 PM: Over the last two hours I answered more e-mail and comments on a break between writing sessions and managed 1,800 words as well in two different writing sessions.

So now, as is normal for me, Walter White Kitty and I are headed for the dark media room downstairs to take a short nap before dinner.

So 1,800 words so far total today.

DAY 4, ENTRY 4:

9:30 PM: Nap and dinner were done around 8:15 and then I answered a few questions and e-mails, did a little work on a workshop, and went back to the writing computer for another session. I managed another 1,000 words or so in an hour.

Now I'm taking a break, going to work on the Pitches and Blurbs workshop with the writers taking that online class, and then go back to writing. That's the plan, anyway. Just under 3,000 words so far today total. About right, especially for a Monday that had a lot of other things going on.

DAY 4, ENTRY 5:

11:30 PM: I spent most of the last two hours working on the Online Workshop Pitches and Blurbs, getting the assignments back to the writers and doing a video response. Then I wrote a quick 500 words and am now heading for the media room to watch The Voice, the best show ever done to show how artists at top levels work and are trained. It's a stunner and a must-see for anyone wanting to be a writer. So much knowledge.

Back after a time.

DAY 4, ENTRY 6:

2:30 AM: I watched all two hours of The Voice. Stunning stuff about art and being an artist. Then I came back up to this computer, did a little more workshop stuff, then went and wrote.

In two sessions with a short break I did around 1,500 more words. So by my rough count I'm in about 5,000 words so far today. I'll add it all up later when I finish tonight. Still got some energy left, surprising on a day like today and all the errands and work and workshop stuff.

DAY 4, ENTRY 7:

4:00 AM: Brain just never got back on it tonight. Too much stuff, too many distractions today, which I had fully expected for a Monday. So I'm heading to the big screen to veg over some bad television and then to bed.

Today I also made it through that deadly one-third spot in any novel (1/3 of 70,000 words is 23,300 words) where the energy is gone, everything seems like a pile a crap, and you lose interest in the book and even writing more. I have never had a novel that I didn't go through that. It's where most beginning novelists stop cold. Professional novelists know about this and just power through.

I went through it today, actually this afternoon. So that feels good as well to have that barrier behind me.

Even though this was a lower word count day, I still feel great about the entire process and feel like I am right on target for an eight or nine day novel without problems. I always have lower word count days, usually the first and fourth days. The next tough day will be Thursday, but I might be on a roll by then, so I'm not going to worry about it now.

Barring unforseens, tomorrow might be my first 10,000 word day. We shall see.

TOTALS:
Day #1—7,625 words
Day #2—7,734 words
Day #3—7,059 words
Day #4—5,070 words
Total so far—27,488 words

DAY FIVE

DAY 5, ENTRY 1:

2:50 PM: Rolled out of bed at 1:20 PM and made it to my computer with my breakfast bars by 1:50 PM. Since then I've been answering comments and e-mails. Folks, the most important part of this is the comments after each day and during the day. I do my best to answer each question honestly. So make sure to read them all. It will be worth your time.

You might discover a myth you didn't even know you were holding.

Now off to my writing computer.
Back later...

DAY 5, ENTRY 2:

6:50 PM: I managed a session of about 900 words, took a break, had a quick lunch that Kris brought back after she had run the errands today. Then I went back and got another 900 words done before Kris and I took off for the grocery store.

I stopped at Goodwill for a few minutes, found nothing, then we went to the store. A bunch of locals were there and we ended up talking for a time, got back around 6:00PM.

At 6:00 PM I sat down for a third afternoon session and got another 900 or so words. Now it's 6:50 PM and I'm headed for the regular nap with my white cat downstairs.

Total so far today about 2,800 words.

DAY 5, ENTRY 3:

10:00 PM: Nap and dinner and news. I think I made it back up here around 8:00 PM. Last two hours I was working on the homework for the essentials workshop and doing the taping of my response to this week's assignment. This was a fun assignment and it was fun to read what the eleven writers in the Essentials workshop turned in this last week.

(I'll do a post about the workshops starting the first week of May and the ones starting the first week of June...still openings in all of them. Under the Online Workshop tab at the top of the page.)

So now it's about 10:00 PM and I'm heading back to my writing computer. Another update after a time…

DAY 5, ENTRY 4:

12:47 AM: I wrote for two sessions, both fairly short from 10:00 until around 11:30 and ended up getting closer to 4,000 words for the day.

At 11:30 PM I went down to the media room to watch The Voice. Then watched a great interview with Carol Burnett and the star of Arrow on The Tonight Show. Now back up here, answering questions and heading back to my writing computer.

It's now 12:51 AM. Need a new cup of tea and then I'm off to writing. We shall see how it goes from here for the rest of the evening…

DAY 5, ENTRY 5:

4:30 AM: I was typing along and I felt I was about halfway done with this book, so I stopped and decided to add it all up. And behold, I am. Good place to stop for the night.

I did three of sessions since 1:00 AM, and did some workshop stuff as well. Each session turned out to be around a thousand words or so. That seems to be normal for me, hitting a stride after midnight or one for a few hours.

So at this point the pace is still nine days for me unless I don't pick up speed or get stuck or have a bad day. If that happens, this will take ten days. (I do plan on picking up speed for the next four days, but we shall see. Some books just don't allow that to happen. But I would love to be done late Saturday night instead of Sunday night.

No reason other than I want to finish putting together *Fiction River* Volume Three: *Time Streams* that I am editing and I have other stories to write.)

TOTALS:
**Day #1—7,625 words
Day #2—7,734 words
Day #3—7,059 words
Day #4—5,070 words
Day #5—7,786 words
Total so far—35,274 words.**

DAY SIX

I'm about halfway to my hoped-for-and-contracted-word-count of 70,000 words. Seemingly right on schedule for my ten day pace. So we shall see how the next half of this goes.

As far as the plot, I still have NO IDEA at all where this is heading. But I am having fun writing it. I know that bothers many people who fear writing into the dark, but at the moment it's great fun for me. The characters are just moving forward and occasionally I get to the end of a chapter or scene and know what needs to be in the next chapter. But that's it. I hope in a few days to have some idea how this will end. I'll let you know when that happens.

Or if I get stuck.

Now off into the second half of the novel and Day 6.

DAY 6, ENTRY 1:

3:30 PM: Rolled out of bed at 1:30 today and got to the Internet computer around 2:15 with my breakfast bars. It's a stunningly beautiful day here today, with the ocean a little rough from a light wind. Last night as I was writing I was sneezing like crazy, driving poor old Walter White Kitty nuts. I'd sneeze and he'd yell at me. Not sure what he was saying, but I know where the sneezing was coming from. I had my office window open and the wind was out of the east, something it rarely is here, so all the crap from the Portland valley was blowing over this way. I must be allergic to something growing over there. Thankfully, today the wind is shifting back off the ocean so there is clean air again like we are used to here.

I had a ton of e-mail and workshop stuff to answer this morning, so it's now 3:30 PM and I'm headed to the writing computer for a session before heading out to WMG Publishing offices and the snail mail.

Later…

DAY 6, ENTRY 2:

4:15 PM: I wrote about 500 words, then realized I was running late and jumped out of here to head for the post office. I then stopped by WMG Publishing and went down and talked to the fine folks at Ella Distribution for a few short minutes, then grabbed some Burger King and came home.

5:00 PM: While eating I heard a noise outside and opened the door to find a long-haired gray cat spooked off the porch and under the car. So I got him/her some food and it came right back up to eat. Clearly hungry. We thought it a neighbor's cat the first few times we saw it, but now we're not so sure anymore. It is thin and too hungry to be a neighbor's

cat. We just hadn't seen it much. So now it looks like I'll be trapping and taking in another cat. Sigh…

5:45 PM: Finally got back to the writing computer after answering a few more e-mails. I got another 1,100 words in. It's now 6:45 and I'm going to head back to another thirty minute writing session before heading down to the media room for a nap with the Waltese Falcon, as Kris calls him.

DAY 6, ENTRY 3:

8:00 PM: I got back up here and started into the homework on the Ideas workshop, working my way slowly through that and then recording the response video for the week. I was finished with that about 10:00. Some great stuff in those assignments, fun reading.

10:00 PM: Finished the workshop homework for the night, answered a few e-mail, and then Kris came in and told me her new blog was done, so I went out to the kitchen and read that. It's a great one, about taking chances. She's talking this week about something we do so normally around here it's like breathing, but most writers don't. In fact, the myths I've been pounding at here in all these comments are about writers afraid to try something new or something they believe "won't work for me." Anyway, it's a great column and it will be up tomorrow morning like normal (Thursday) on her site, so read it, folks.

10:30 PM: headed back to my writing computer as soon as I get a cup of tea. Not sure how far in I am today. I think I'm past a couple thousand words, not great, but considering the day, not bad. I'll add it up later.

Now Available
from all your favorite booksellers
in trade paper and electronic editions.

USA TODAY BESTSELLING AUTHOR

DEAN WESLEY SMITH

HEINLEIN'S
RULES

FIVE SIMPLE
BUSINESS RULES
FOR WRITING

A WMG WRITER'S GUIDE

DAY 6, ENTRY 4:

11:45 PM: Taking a short break. Back later with a writing update...

DAY 6, ENTRY 5:

1:45 AM: Not a clue how much I have done, but it doesn't feel like enough. For some reason really tired tonight. I haven't lost the will to live yet, but there is no doubt I am dragging on this book at the moment.

Might have something to do with the fact that I still don't have a clue where this thing is going. Or that I ended up doing far too many other things today, including just spending an hour plus watching television instead of writing.

So now I'm going to go back to my writing computer and do what I tell other writers to do: Write the next line.

I'll be back later with the end of the day numbers and such.

DAY 6, ENTRY 6:

4:15 AM: I'm giving up, even though I have a hunch I could go farther tonight and do another session, another 800 words. I just flat don't feel like it, so headed for the basement to watch some really bad television, then go to bed.

Somehow in the last few hours I managed to write another 2,500 words or so, so the day ended up better than I had expected when I added it all up. I had over 2,000 words done before I went for a nap, dinner, and then did the homework for the online workshop. And it seems I did another 2,500 or so words before going down to watch some television earlier.

Then I managed another 2,500 or so in the last few sessions, with five minute breaks and doing about 800 or so words per session. So maybe this is picking up speed a little.

If I can get a fairly clear day on Thursday, Friday, and Saturday, I still might finish this in nine days. Again, we shall see because I still don't know where it's going. But I am getting there at a decent and pretty consistent clip. (grin)

TOTALS:
Day #1—7,625 words
Day #2—7,734 words
Day #3—7,059 words
Day #4—5,070 words
Day #5—7,786 words
Day #6—7,116 words
Total so far—42,380 words.

And that, folks, is how you write a short novel in 6 days.

You ever wonder how writers like Lester Dent (Doc Savage), Max Brand, and other pulp writers and mystery writers in the fifties and sixties did it, that was how. Take one day off and start again. Four short novels a month. And I taught workshops and did a bunch of other stuff at the same time.

And got full night's sleep every night.

Now onward to a novel of 70,000 words because that what this stupid contract says and I still don't have a climax, let alone an ending. But I will. I will.

I trust the process.

DAY SEVEN

DAY 7, ENTRY 1:

2:30 PM: Rolled out of bed by 1:15 PM today and was in here with my breakfast bars by 1:45. Now done with e-mail and comments, so headed to the writing computer before Kris comes get me to head out for errands and lunch and shopping and such.

Back with a word count later…

DAY 7, ENTRY 2:

10:30 PM: Wow, does this day suck so far. Yes, that time is 10:30 PM: late in the evening…I have about 1,200 words done so far and haven't done the homework yet for the workshop. So off to do that next, then back to the book.

Just too much business stuff today. Sigh…Kris and I went out for errands, had lunch, I wrote a little, she wrote a little, and then business all evening. Now back in my office. And somehow I need to get my mind back on this book. (grin)

DAY 7, ENTRY 3:

2:30 AM: Well, this day is a great example of life getting in the way. After that last entry even more business came up and had to be worked through and talked about. But I did get the homework done for the workshop and all that.

I think I have around 1,500 words done so far today, but going to get back at this now and see what I can manage. I fully expected to do upwards of 10,000

words today…yeah…so much for expectations…(grin) Just far, far too much business stuff I'm afraid.

So, not only is this an example of how to write regularly, it's an example of how to work through life being tossed at you.

Now over to the writing computer and see if I can remember where I was before all this crap hit the fan…

DAY 7, ENTRY 4:

4:00 AM: Two fairly intense sessions of about 700 words each session, both lasting about forty minutes, and I'm burnt to a crisp after today.

I'm going to go watch some bad television and then go to bed.

TOTALS:
Day #1—7,625 words
Day #2—7,734 words
Day #3—7,059 words
Day #4—5,070 words
Day #5—7,786 words
Day #6—7,116 words
Day #7—3,005 words
Total so far—45,385 words.
(Just over 24,000 words to go…)

I'm stunned I even managed those two sessions today to be honest. With luck, tomorrow will be a better day and I'll be back on track. Stay tuned.

I promised you I would be honest with the word count and the days and what happens to a point. It suppose it was too much to ask from life for me to get an open nine or ten days of writing without business crashing in and throwing around a few fun things to deal with. But they are dealt with for the moment, now back to writing for the weekend.

Still aiming for Sunday and ten days on this.

DAY EIGHT

DAY 8, ENTRY 1:

5:30 PM: Rolled out of bed by 1:30 PM today and was in here with my breakfast bars by 2:00 PM. I managed to get some of my e-mail and stuff done here, but then got called away into business meetings with a business lawyer and then I had lunch with Kris and stopped up at WMG for a time.

Now back here.

I'm going to do a little more e-mail and such and then shift over to the writing chair and get going on the book, work to have a good day if not a great day on it. Yeah, I know, starting late today, but it's Friday night and I'm old and got nothing better to do but write.

DAY 8, ENTRY 2:

7:15 PM: Well, I'm back on a roll again. In two sessions with only a few minute break between them, I managed almost 2,500 words in just under two hours. Now that's rocket speed for me. (Pent up typing I guess.)

And in the middle of it my subconscious tossed in a nasty plot twist that will take some pages to resolve, but I guess my subconscious was telling me I didn't have enough book.

Who knows. I just trust the process and try to stay out of the way.

I'm sure all of you out there are having a good Friday night. Watching a person like me write would be like watching paint dry. Only way watching paint dry would be fun would be with a lot of booze, some loud music, and lots of great friends. And the wet paint would have to be on someone you find attractive. (grin)

But I'm here alone, I don't drink anymore, and my oldies station is turned down low. Kris is buried in writing the new Smokey Dalton novel, so she's living in 1970. So I think I'll live for a time longer in the book I'm writing.

That said, however, the sun is streaming in over the Pacific right now, making this office far too bright for a night person like me. So I'm grabbing the cat and heading for a nap.

Back later…

DAY 8, ENTRY 3:

9:30 PM: Fed, nap, and watched the news. Ready to fire again. Now just have to shift Walter White Kitty from napping on my writing chair to napping on this Internet chair and I can get writing again.

No writing workshop homework tonight, so just straight back to writing…

DAY 8, ENTRY 4:

11:30 PM: Two sessions since 9:30 with a quick run to the store between them. I managed another 2,000 words bringing the total to pretty close to 4,500 so far today.

Interesting as I was headed to the grocery store around 10:15, it felt like when I would head out to the casino about that time of night on a Friday night. Over the years that was my favorite time to play poker since the rookies were drinking and getting tired and were tossing money around like it was something they didn't care about. I would come in, join the table, and take their money for a few hours and be home by three in the morning.

Felt weird going out like that again and not going to the casino.

On the book side of things, I finally figured out the ending and climax. Yeah!! About 18,000 to 20,000 words left to write, so pretty much on target and I think the climax of the book and the ending will take in that word range to write.

I actually was starting to get a little worried earlier as my subconscious snuck in a nifty plot twist which felt like it would take a lot of words to write. The very LAST thing I want is a work-for-hire novel being one word longer than what they are paying me for.

So now off to a break to watch a little television, then back for more words. I will report in a couple more times tonight.

DAY 8, ENTRY 5:

2:30 AM: Give or take…watched too much television tonight. Not sure why, just felt like it on a Friday night. More than likely because I figured out the ending and now I'm bored. Sigh…

I'm still just under 5,000 words for the day. Better get going so I can finish this thing on Sunday. Get it turned in on Monday.

DAY 8, ENTRY 6:

5:30 AM: Give or take…got tired an hour or so back and gave up and went back to watch bad television. So didn't turn out to be a great day, just an okay day.

TOTALS:
Day #1—7,625 words
Day #2—7,734 words
Day #3—7,059 words
Day #4—5,070 words
Day #5—7,786 words
Day #6—7,116 words
Day #7—3,005 words
Day #8—7,473 words
Total so far—52,858 words.

(Just over 17,000 words to go…and I know where I am going now and am bored…sigh…I hate knowing the ending of something I am writing…)

DAY NINE

DAY 9, ENTRY 1:

4:45 PM: Horrid slow start on this fine Saturday. Managed to get out of bed later than normal and have been doing e-mail and working on business stuff with Kris. Of course this turned out to be a week of major business things. Figures….

I should be at this after I head out for a quick lunch, then back here for some writing.

DAY 9, ENTRY 2:

7:30 PM: I went out to the auction and had a great time working with the owner there over some collectables, then grabbed myself some lunch and the mail, then got back here and did two quick sessions. So far around 1,800 words total for the day.

Now off to nap with the cat.

DAY 9, ENTRY 3:

11:00 PM: The ending on this caused me to make a major change in the plot, so I went back to the beginning and changed that detail and wrote some new scenes and such around that one major detail shift. Then ran forward, so about 2,000 new words since about 9 PM, plus the changes.

No, that was not rewriting, that was a detail shift that was required by something I found two hundred pages later, that required new words inserted in a few places up in the front of the book. That is what I call "cycling" or "fixing."

If I wrote like Kris writes, she would have made a note and kept typing forward and then gone back on a "fix" draft and put that in. But since I am mailing this book tomorrow night to the editor, I needed to fix it now, the moment I realized the needed detail insertion.

Note: the reader getting to the end will think the author was brilliant because he could plant such information and have it turn up later in the book. Or they will think the author must have really outlined the book to make sure such information was up front that was needed later.

I am not brilliant nor did I outline. I'm just not afraid of going back and adding in a detail. No big deal.

Powering forward...

DAY 9, ENTRY 4:

1:45 AM: I did another thousand words, then went up to WMG Offices and dinged around up there for a time because I just felt like I needed to for no reason at all that I could think of. Then came back,

watched an hour of news and television, now back up here in my office for the rest of the evening.

Seems this book is just not speeding up or slowing down. Just normal days dinging along on this.

I'm around 5,000 words so far today, so we shall see how this ends up.

DAY 9, ENTRY 5:

3:30 AM: I did another couple thousand words in just under two hours, with one short break to get something to drink.

Still going...night not finished yet.

DAY 9, ENTRY 6:

6:30 AM: I'm up a little late tonight. Wrote until after 5, then went and watched some bad television.

Managed about 2,500 more words. Total for the day is 9,373 words.

TOTALS:
Day #1—7,625 words
Day #2—7,734 words
Day #3—7,059 words
Day #4...5,070 words
Day #5—7,786 words
Day #6—7,116 words
Day #7—3,005 words
Day #8—7,473 words
Day #9—9,373 words
Total so far—62,231 words.
Within sight...

DAY TEN

DAY 10, ENTRY 1:

4:45 PM: Normal Sunday start today. Got up around 1:00 PM, managed some e-mail before heading off to the professional writer's lunch at 2:00 PM. Got back around 3:45 PM and am now done with e-mail and comments for the moment.

So headed toward my writing computer to get a session done. Later tonight I need to do a few hours on the online workshop that I am teaching called Cliffhangers. I need to get letters about assignments back to everyone and my in general response recorded.

But even with that and the lunch today, I don't see much worry about finishing tonight. I seem to be powering right along just fine and dandy. Ending is in sight and it seems to be coming in close enough to the 70,000 word number to make my editor happy in New York.

We shall see when the day is over what the actual number will be.

I want to thank you all as well for the great comments and questions. If you haven't read all the questions and comments on every day, you want to make sure you do that. You never know what tiny bit of information from somewhere will help you with your own writing.

Now off to write and finish this novel so I can get started on something of my own again, plus I have at least three short stories editors are waiting for.

DAY 10, ENTRY 2:

6:45 PM: Managed just over 2,000 words in the last two hours. Firing right along now toward the ending...

Now off to the standard nap. White cat is waiting for me at the top of the stairs pretending to be asleep.

DAY 10, ENTRY 3:

10:00 PM: I had a nap and dinner and then came back here to my office and worked on the homework assignments for the Cliffhanger workshop, then did the video here in my office as well for that workshop. Too lazy at the moment to go up to the WMG Publishing offices where I normally record the videos.

So now, with the homework done, e-mails mostly answered, I'm headed back to my writing computer. Make a run at the end of this thing so I can get all my chapter files combined into one file and the entire novel sent off to the New York editor. And then they will owe me money again, which, of course, knowing traditional publishers as well as I do, won't arrive until August and then only after I scream for a time.

Ahh, I hate that part of this business.

Back to the fun part, the writing.

DAY 10, ENTRY 4:

11:00 PM: Taking a break...powered out about 1,200 words in an hour before needing to stop for five minutes. This much faster pace is normal for me near the end of a book. Not sure if I write more because I want the stupid thing over, or I write more because I'm bored and need to go fast to get finished.

3,200 approximately done for the day so far, plus lunch with writers and all the homework done for the workshop I'm teaching.

On schedule…

Not a clue how much more.

Back to typing…

DAY 10, ENTRY 5:

12:15 AM: another 1,000 words done before another break.

DAY 10, ENTRY 6:

2:30 AM: Done.

TOTALS:
Day #1—7,625 words
Day #2—7,734 words
Day #3—7,059 words
Day #4—5,070 words
Day #5—7,786 words
Day #6—7,116 words
Day #7—3,005 words
Day #8—7,473 words
Day #9—9,373 words
Day #10—6,719 words
Total—68,950 words.

I still have to spend fifteen minutes and combine it into one file and fire it off to the editor. But the writing is done.

The ending worked out fine and came quickly, as I expected. I'm slightly under the 70,000 words asked for in the contract, but not enough to worry about.

Ten days, pretty normal days for me, actually. I taught the online workshops, did a ton of business, read, watched

television, and mostly got full nights sleep each night.

In other words, I did nothing different this week except do more blog posts than I normally would do and answer more comments than I normally answer in a week. But that was fun as well.

Remember, the total is only original fiction words in the last ten days. It does not count hundreds of e-mails, all the workshop letters in the workshops I am teaching, or all the comments answered in these posts. I don't count any of that, or these blogs either which were just over 1,000 words each for ten days.

The only thing important to a fiction writer like me is new fiction words.

I hope this exercise was worth the time for those of you watching. It wasn't much unusual for me except that this novel contract allowed me to do this.

Good luck everyone fighting the myths that stop you.

Writing really is fun. If you let it be fun.

THE DAY AFTER

I just finished close to a 70,000 words on a novel I was hired to do by a New York publisher. Did it in ten days here and blogged about my days and how I did the words. The editor on the book reported that it arrived just fine.

Someone local came up to me today and congratulated me on finishing the book and I said, "Congratulations on going to work today." I do not think the person understood.

Thanks everyone for the very kind thank-you comments on this. And numbers of people seemed stunned that I could go to work for ten days, then go to work on day #11. So for one more day, I'll do my day here. Just to try to put one more nail in the attempt at killing a few ugly myths about how writers work.

Now for one more day of watching paint dry.

THE DAY AFTER, ENTRY 1:

8:30 PM: Horrid start to the day, but alas I'm back here. A couple of the days in the novel writing I didn't get into the office until late to write, so back at this like normal.

The day started early for me as well, getting up around 12:00, getting my three breakfast bars eaten while doing some e-mail and then heading to the WMG offices by 1:30 PM. Meetings on all sorts of business stuff, then Kris and I had lunch and I went back for more meeting from 4 until 6:00 PM.

Then I went down to a local restaurant to enjoy part of a birthday celebration for a friend, then to the grocery store and back home to cook Kris dinner. We watched the news, I came up here to my office, worked on e-mail and did this. I will now work on the homework for the online workshop I am teaching called Pitches and Blurbs, then head back to the WMG Offices for a time.

I expect to be back here in my office at home by around 11:00 PM and headed for the writing computer. Up at WMG Publishing tonight I'll work on putting together *Fiction River: Time Streams* that I am editing so I can get that turned in on time. When I get back here I'll tell you what I end up writing on and give page counts.

THE DAY AFTER, ENTRY 2:

10:35 PM: Back from the WMG Publishing offices. Got my response recorded up there tonight for the workshop and got it loaded to the workshop site, then ended up spending thirty minutes talking with the landlord, who has a shop in the back of the building and is never there at night. He's a great guy.

So didn't work on the *Fiction River* editing, but instead came back here, did some more workshop work, now headed for my writing computer. At some point I'll go downstairs to watch The Voice. (As I have said before, a writer can learn a ton from this show if you understand what you are watching.)

THE DAY AFTER, ENTRY 3:

2:15 AM: I worked for about 45 minutes at a new Jukebox short story for Time Streams anthology, got about 600 words in, took a break and a short nap on the couch outside my office. Kris woke me up twenty minutes later and we went and watched The Voice and Castle.

Now I'm back in my office and headed back to the short story. Again, a slow start today because of all the business stuff, but still pretty normal. Tomorrow will be back to normal because I have ZERO meetings scheduled. (grin)

THE DAY AFTER, ENTRY 4 (THE LAST):

3:00 AM: I finally decided I'm done with this experiment to blog about my writing of a ghost novel. So this is the last entry, even though I will be up for a time longer writing.

I finished another 700 words or so on the time travel story. Title at the moment is Home is a Song. That might change, but so far it is fitting.

I'll keep going and get it done tonight or tomorrow, but not going to post the words or anything here.

I also have a thriller I wrote that I need to dig out of my files and get turned into WMG Publishing by Wednesday so it can get into the proof and production stages, so going to do that tomorrow. (Not rewrite, just dig it out and turn it in. A book called "Dead Money" already written, never sold.)

I have a new blog post coming on things in indie publishing on Thursday or Friday in my New World of Publishing series. I've been working on that in spare moments and I think it might be something a lot of writers have not thought about, but since it wasn't fiction, I didn't count it any more than I counted these.

So that's it. After 11 days of this silliness, back to regularly scheduled posts...I have writing to do...

Ghost of a Chance Series Available...

Now Available
from all your favorite booksellers
in trade paper and electronic editions.
The first Cold Poker Gang novel.

Smith's
STORIES

DEAN WESLEY SMITH
A *USA Today* Bestselling Writer
PROFILE GAP
A Thunder Mountain Short Story

Institute traveler, Sharon Kent, wants to keep a man who existed in the past alive. She likes him, and they had set a date for dinner before he was killed.

But in timeline after timeline, she keeps going back to find out what happened to him. Finally, she discovers he died in a mine cave-in in every timeline. And thus always stood her up for their date.

But this time, with the help of Duster Kendal, she hopes to rescue him.

And maybe then he will make their date.

PROFILE GAP
A Thunder Mountain Story

ONE

SHARON KENT sat on her horse, tucked back into the shade of a stand of tall pine along the edge of Profile Creek. The August sun was beating down into the mountain valley, making the air smell like hot pine and making her drink a lot more water than normal.

Down the valley was Profile Lake, just about as beautiful a small mountain lake as there could be. She had camped on its banks a few times. Profile Gap valley was fairly wide in this area in comparison to many valleys in these central Idaho mountains. Often valleys in this area were no more than fifty paces wide walls of rock that led up to towering mountain peaks.

Profile Gap was actually like a wide meadow and if it hadn't been so high, she would have had no doubt a mining town would have sprang up here. A small one, trying to service the miners in the area was attempting to catch hold, but it only had a small general store and a post office and she knew from her studies in the future that was all it would ever be.

Sharon had on her normal riding clothes for a woman of means of this time. Dark slacks, a white silk blouse with a dark vest over it, and leather riding boots. She always topped off the outfit with a wide-brimmed hat that kept the sun off her face.

All her clothes had been made in the future and were comfortable and allowed her to breathe and stay moderately cool, even in the heat of a mountain summer day.

This was the fifth time she had followed Eugene Walls up to this high mountain valley. The first two times she had lost him even though she had figured out where exactly he was heading and how he would die.

It seems he had a mine just down the valley from her on the right wall of the valley, tucked just up a small stream. He was in that mine now and in fifteen minutes the entire thing would collapse on him.

Actually, the mouth of the mine would collapse, trapping him in the back where he eventually would die of lack of oxygen after what she and a couple institute scientists figured was at least four days.

So if she did this right, today she might be able to rescue him.

Camped down by Profile Lake was Duster Kendal and four others. They were part of the work crew that had built the Monumental Summit lodge and loved working for Duster, since he paid so well.

It was going to be dangerous work to rescue Eugene.

And she had no idea why she had wanted to, actually.

Eugene was a handsome man for this time, about her age at thirty, with a wide smile, great teeth, and dark brown eyes that matched his dark hair. He had been a

lawyer back east before coming out to try his hand finding gold.

She was attracted to him and found him wonderful company.

He had been attracted to her as well. She stood five seven, just two inches shorter than he was, and her hair was almost the same color brown, as were her eyes.

One person actually asked if they were brother and sister they matched so well. After that time, she had gone back to 2018 to make sure that they hadn't actually been related in any fashion. From what little she could find about him, they were not, thankfully.

They had had a date for dinner in six days, but in other timelines he never arrived and was never seen again. The first time he stood her up, she had gone back to 2018 to try to do research and figure out what had happened to him.

She was a psychologist with a specialty and area of interest of the relationships of the pioneers. So she had almost no experience in deep historical research past the family trees of families she ended up getting to know in the past.

But with the help from a few of the institute historical librarians, they had discovered Eugene had a mining claim in Profile Gap and worked it regularly all summer, returning to his ranch outside of Boise to stay every few weeks. But there were no records of why he vanished.

He had left a large sum of money as well in two of the Boise banks that went unclaimed for decades, as well as his mining claim and his small ranch on the Boise River.

She had originally met him at breakfast at the Idanha Hotel and he was a perfect gentleman. And funny. So with every timeline, she would go meet him again, try to get more information out of him as to what might cause his vanishing act.

And when that didn't work, she decided to just follow him, using high-powered binoculars from the future to stay far enough back that he would never notice her.

The last two times she got ahead of him and watched him ride up the little side valley to his mine and then watch the dust fly from the mine's collapse.

She so wanted to stop him, but she could figure out no way to do that without telling him she knew he would die in there.

So she had talked with Duster and Bonnie.

Duster actually knew Eugene from playing poker with him, so they had decided to dig up the mine in 2018. There they found his mummified remains, curled up as if he had gone to sleep. He clearly had tried to dig his way out, without success.

The image of his remains just curled up there on the mine floor haunted her. That was not how Eugene Walls was supposed to end his days.

Duster got some geological engineers in the future to tell him how to safely open that cave-in back up to rescue Eugene.

And now, back here in 1904, that was what they were going to do.

All because she wanted that date with Eugene.

Damn silly and she knew it, but Duster and Bonnie hadn't thought it was. Then they spent some time telling her how saving him would create brand new timelines, but in their timeline, the one she left from in 2017, he would always be dead in that mine.

And since there was an infinite number of timelines, why not create some

with him alive where she might have a chance at that date?

She took another long drink of water and watched in the direction of Eugene's mine. Right on time the ground rumbled and a puff of dust rose into the air and dissipated quickly.

And that was that.

Eugene Walls was trapped and would die in a few days if they didn't dig him out.

She turned her horse back to the trail following along the stream toward the lake. Duster and the rest would be ready.

And when they did get Eugene out, she had no idea what to say to him. She certainly couldn't tell him she had stared at his mummified remains in 2018.

Or that she thought him handsome and fun and wanted to save his life for a date.

She had no idea what she was going to say.

TWO

AS DUSTER had told her, once he and the five he brought along from the Monumental Lodge crew got started digging and using timbers to shore up the sides and roof, it wouldn't take much time. Actually, they were able to open up the slide in five hours.

As they cleared the last rock, Sharon heard Eugene say from inside the mine, "Oh, thank God."

Duster helped him through the small hole and out into the chill of the late evening air. Sharon had set them up a camp on a small flat just below the mine and had food cooking for all of them.

But when Eugene came out of the mine, she was standing there smiling.

Eugene shook Duster's hand, then each of the other men, before even noticing Sharon.

He looked shocked. Then he smiled, the dirt covering his face making him even more handsome if that was possible.

He moved to her as the men gathered up their equipment and put it back in their saddlebags.

"Thank you," he said, taking her hand.

The feeling of his hand against hers sent tingles through her body and she just nodded.

"I assume I have you to thank for this rescue," he said. "Since you were following me."

She smiled. "I didn't know I was following you."

Sharon had a story about visiting a friend in Edwardsburg and was just riding this way. She had caught up with him as he turned toward his mine. But she would save that story for later."

"How did you find Duster and his crew?"

"We were just camped down by the lake," Duster said, rescuing Sharon. "Coming in from Monumental Summit and heading down to Edwardsburg and onto the Big Creek drainage."

"My lucky day all the way around," Eugene said.

"Thank her," Duster said. "She was the one who saw the dust from the cave-in, saw your horse tied up by a camp and figured out what had happened and went to find help. Lucky you weren't caught in the rock fall."

Eugene glanced back at the mine. "Yeah, I think my mining days are done. Not getting anything out of that death trap anyhow."

"Well," Sharon said, "If you all want to get cleaned up down in the creek, I have a large stew cooking and some bread that I brought from the Monumental Lodge I will be glad to share."

Eugene smiled and nodded and once again said, "Thank you."

Then he and the others went to wash up while she tried to calm her racing heart and actually figure out how to serve six hungry men.

She was a psychologist, not a camp chef.

But at least now Eugene would have a chance at living a full life.

And they might just get that date.

With luck, more than one.

~

Thunder Mountain Novels Available...

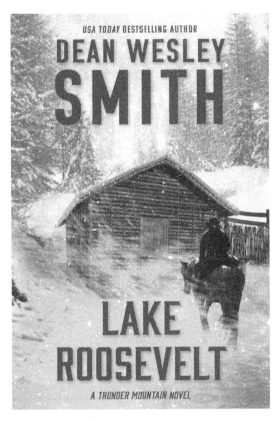

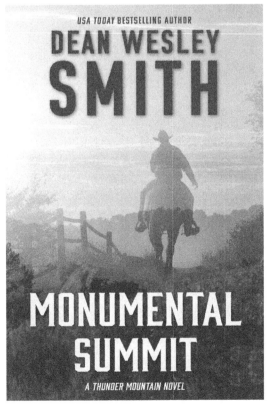

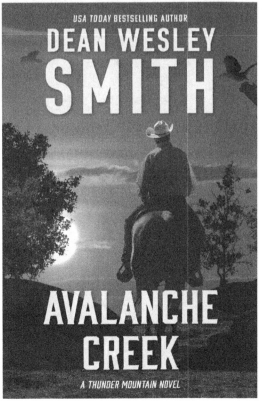

Smith's
STORIES

DEAN WESLEY SMITH
CAT IN THE AIR
A Pahket Jones Short Story

I always wanted to create a character in my Poker Boy universe who dealt with cats. Kris and I deciding to do a series of twelve cat anthologies gave me the perfect chance.

And people love the anthology series, **The Year of the Cat**. *Twelve volumes with 100 cat stories.*

Superhero Pakhet Jones deals with all things cats. Her job and she loves it.

And in this story, Pakhet faces a conundrum only a cat can create.

CAT IN THE AIR
A Pakhet Jones Story

ONE

THE LARGE, BLACK TUXEDO CAT sat calmly on an eight-inch window ledge nine stories in the air. The cat didn't crouch or even act afraid, although it didn't move. It just sat there like it perched nine stories in the air every day, calmly looking around. Problem was that none of the windows in that area of the condo building opened. Not on that floor or the floor above or below it.

And there were no balconies close at all.

None.

Behind the cat was an expanse of dark window and heat radiated off the glass and the building in shimmers.

I had no idea how the cat got there, but it just looked around like it owned the entire downtown area of Las Vegas on this hot summer afternoon.

My name is Pakhet Jones and I am a superhero in the world of cats. Honestly, I just don't think I am, that is actually my job, and has been now for well over a hundred years. I work in the world of cats. Big cats, small house cats, you name it, I work with them and often save their lives or the lives of their owners.

Or as cats like to call them, their companions. Cats refuse to be owned. Can't say as I blame them.

I had just teleported into my condo in the Ogden and had changed into my skimpy bikini to head to my "office" at The Beach in the Mandalay Resort and Casino. My office on beautiful sunny days was an air-conditioned cabana on the sand, looking out over the water and waves and tourists that filled the large pool area. I loved to lie in the sun there just like any cat. As a superhero of cats, I also had a lot of their traits, something I didn't mind at all.

Around me my condo was bright, with light brown shades and white cabinets and off-white walls. I liked light and brightness and my two-bedroom condo reflected that.

I had just put on my cover-up, a thin silk robe that didn't cover much of anything, and was about to jump to the women's room at the Mandalay Resort when I heard a faint, *Little help would be appreciated.*

Now I can hear a cat's thoughts when they are directed at me. Can't hear people's thoughts, thankfully, but I can hear cats. Just one of my many superpowers.

And I can sort of tell from which direction the cat's thoughts were coming. So I went outside onto my balcony on the 14th floor looking over the City of Las Vegas and looked down and there was the black and white tom cat.

"How in the world did you get there?" I asked out loud, directing my question at the cat.

I just did.

Typical cat response.

I studied the ledge the cat sat on. It was very narrow, not much larger than the cat, and ended in two concrete pillars on either side. Basically it was a window ledge to a set of massive windows of a condo. But those windows did not open.

And who knew who lived behind those windows and if they were home.

At this point that ledge had to be getting very warm, considering the temperature at the moment was climbing past 100 degrees and was scheduled to top out over 110 this afternoon. That black and white cat stood no chance in that direct sunlight and heat for much longer than another hour, if that.

And more than likely the cat knew it, which was why it asked for help. Cats, by their very nature, hate asking for help under any circumstances. I understood that trait as well.

I studied the ledge as best I could. I could teleport down to the cat, pick him up and teleport back up here before I fell off, but I would be visible to anyone who was looking that way for the few seconds it took me to pick up the cat.

I didn't like that at all. That had to be a last resort. Since I was tall and very thin and had deep golden skin and a completely bald head, I was very recognizable. Especially wearing a bikini and a sheer cover-up.

I was going to need to find a way to get that cat off the ledge without being seen. And I had to do it soon.

I looked off to the right of the cat and a floor down to where a handsome guy with broad shoulders wearing a deep blue dress shirt sat sipping a drink on his deck, shaded by an overhang. He seemed to be talking to two others in empty chairs, and I realized who I was looking at.

That was Canyon Stevens, a superhero working in the area of business. From what I had heard, he was living here in the Ogden as well with two ghost agents named Marble Grant and Sims.

For years I doubted such things as ghost agents existed, but lately stories I had heard from trusted friends told how ghost agents had helped Poker Boy and his team save the world a couple of times.

I had never met a ghost agent. There were a lot of things in my hundred years as a superhero that I hadn't done.

Someday, I also really hoped to meet Poker Boy, but a superhero in the world of cats didn't often cross paths with a superhero in the world of poker. But at times I caught glimmerings of his office hanging out in mid-air above the Strip.

"Be right back with help," I thought at the cat.

Do not be long.

That was not a good sign. Cats did not get impatient unless their lives were on the line. Clearly this cat knew the heat would hurt him very soon.

TWO

I TELEPORTED to the air-conditioned empty hallway in front of Canyon Steven's condo and rang the bell.

It took a moment, but finally one of the most handsome men I had ever seen opened the door and smiled. I looked right into his deep blue eyes since he was as tall as I was.

Damn that smile of his could melt a woman even on a winter's day in five feet of snow.

I flat blushed like a teenager. Now I like women and men both. But no woman could hold a candle to this guy.

And I was suddenly wishing I had put something on beside the bikini and sheer cover-up. Not that I was ashamed of my body, but appropriate dress just didn't seem to be a bikini in a condo hallway.

"Yes?" he asked, his voice as deep as you would expect from someone so damned good-looking. And he kept smiling. I had to give him credit, though. He kept his gaze locked on mine instead of taking in the sights I was offering below my chin.

"I'm looking for Canyon Stevens."

"You found him," he said, reaching out his hand to shake mine.

I shook his hand and through the hot flash that seemed to cover my entire body I managed to speak. I was damn proud of that accomplishment.

"Pakhet Jones," I said. "Everyone calls me Pak. I am a superhero in the world of cats and I am looking for a little help in rescuing a cat. I also live in this building and saw you sitting on the balcony just below and to the side of where the cat is stuck."

Canyon's smile turned into a look of worry. "We got a cat on a ledge above us?"

I nodded and managed to take a deep breath to calm my heart. I never had had a reaction to a man like that. Very, very strange.

"How in the world did it manage to get up there?"

"It wouldn't tell me," I said.

"Come on in," he said as he turned and headed back across the living room and toward the condo's patio door.

I followed him and as he reached the patio he said, "This is Pakhet Jones, a superhero in the world of cats."

I was guessing he was talking with Marble Grant and Sims, but I could not see or hear them.

He indicated that I should come out on the balcony and point to where the cat was.

I did. You could barely see the big black and white guy from this angle. He clearly had lain down.

"I could jump to the ledge and get him," I said, "but no telling who is inside that condo or who in the city would see me for the few seconds I am there. Too many cameras these days. So I want to leave that as a last resort."

"Yeah, I could get him as well, but would have the same problem," Canyon said, nodding.

He glanced around at the street below, then pointed. "A few people have already seen him up here."

"Damn," I said. "And he will not survive until night. The temperature on that ledge is brutal. I don't think he'll make it another hour."

Canyon turned to an empty area on the deck, listened for a moment, then nodded.

"Marble and Sims can't pick the cat up as ghosts," he said. "Beyond their limits."

I smiled at the empty space on the deck. "Thanks anyway. What I was hoping is if the three of you knew of any kind of shield that could make me invisible for the few seconds I would need on that ledge? Just not one of my powers."

"Not mine either," Canyon said. Then he glanced at the empty space again, then nodded and turned back to me.

"Poker Boy can stop time."

That was not the sentence I had expected him to say.

THREE

THE IDEA of involving Poker Boy in rescuing a cat seemed just damned silly to me. He tended to save people and the world from what I had heard. And he was the only superhero who had his own floating office over the city, that much I knew for sure. He had become sort of the superhero of superheroes and I understood that he and his team worked regularly with Lady Luck herself.

I had never met Lady Luck, the woman in charge of everything. Someday I wished to do that as well.

"Thanks," Canyon said to the empty space where the two ghost agents were.

Then he indicated we should go back inside, picking up his glass as he went. "Marble and Sims have jumped to talk to Patty. See if she can contact Poker Boy."

"Poker Boy's girlfriend?"

Canyon nodded and went over behind the kitchen counter and refilled his glass with water from the fridge door. "Would you like a glass or bottle of water?"

"Glass would be great," I said, moving to sit at the kitchen counter. I could feel the clock ticking on that poor guy on the ledge. I needed to tell him we were working to save him.

"Excuse me for a moment," I said and went back out onto the patio. Then I said into the air in the direction of the cat, "We have help coming."

I do not have much longer, the cat thought back.

"Just hold on a few minutes longer."

The cat said nothing, so I turned and went back inside.

"How is he doing?" Canyon asked, looking very worried.

"Bad," I said. "I'm going to jump to get him no matter who sees me if we can't find help in a few minutes."

"That bad, huh?" a voice said from behind me.

I turned to the smiling face of a young guy wearing a black leather coat and Fedora-like black hat. Why anyone would wear a black leather coat when the temperature was over a hundred was beyond me.

"They call me Poker Boy," he said, smiling and extending his hand.

"Pakhet Jones," I said. "Pak to most everyone. Superhero in the cat world. Got a big tuxedo cat stuck on a ledge above us and to the right. Need to find a way to jump to the ledge without being seen and get him in the next few minutes. The heat on that ledge is going to kill him very soon."

"Well then, let's go get him," Poker Boy said, smiling and turning toward the balcony with a smile and a wave at Canyon.

"Not sure both of us will fit on that ledge," I said, following him.

Poker Boy laughed. "Oh, trust me, I have no intention of going out on that ledge. Heights like this just make me all twisted up."

"So what can I do to not be seen?" I asked, pointing to the ledge where I could still barely see the cat.

"I have this really amazing and fun power to slip between moments of time," Poker Boy said. "Sort of form a bubble where people inside the bubble can move, but the rest of the world doesn't."

"That would be fun," I said, trying to imagine that.

"Comes in real handy at times," Poker Boy said. "I'm thinking we slip between a moment of time, then jump into the condo near the cat. Owners in there will never know we are there."

"Can you hold the bubble outside the window and I jump out and get the cat?"

"Should work," Poker Boy said. He looked down at the people below who were pointing upward at the cat. "To all of them the cat will just vanish when I release the time bubble."

"Thank you," I said.

He laughed. "Don't thank me yet. We got to rescue the guy first. Ready?"

I nodded and an instant later all sound stopped completely. The sounds of the city, the wind, everything.

Nothing was moving, including Canyon who was in stride toward the balcony inside the condo.

Creepy. Damned creepy.

"I'll jump us into the condo near the cat," Poker Boy said and a moment later we were in a condo with green furniture, dark paint on the walls, and way too much pink in the kitchen.

No one seemed to be home.

"Wow, looks like some interior decorator had a really bad day in here," Poker Boy said, looking around.

I had to agree completely.

The black cat was leaning against the window.

I stepped over near the cat, then turned so I was leaning down as if to pick him up and put my feet into a position my right in front of my left. I hoped that would give me enough time on the ledge to get the cat.

Then I teleported onto the ledge.

My shoulders hit the glass and my balance was not there and I was tipping off the ledge.

Somehow I managed to grab the cat. Somehow.

Then falling, I teleported back inside

the condo, landing on the hardwood floor on my side, holding the big cat in my arms.

"Wow, not a chance could I have done that," Poker Boy said. "Not a chance. You all right?"

"I am," I said, again wishing I had spent the moment to put on better clothes for cat rescuing.

The big cat in my arms felt limp as I stood and Poker Boy jumped us down into Canyon's apartment and released the time bubble.

The sounds of the city, the air conditioning, everything slammed back into me and the cat tensed in my arms.

"Canyon, can I get a bowl of water for this guy?"

Canyon stopped in mid-stride going toward the empty balcony and then turned around. "That is really something," he said, shaking his head.

A moment later I had the big tuxedo drinking some water and laying on a cool tile floor in the dining room in the shade. Looked like he was going to make it.

"Thank you," I said to Poker Boy.

He laughed. "My pleasure. I now get to add cat rescuer to my résumé, even though you did all the work. And it has been my pleasure meeting you, Pak. That was some bit of balance and tightrope walking you did there."

"I fell off," I said, laughing.

"Still damned amazing," Poker Boy said. "Now if you will excuse me, I got a great game going at the Bellagio I got to get back to. Canyon, Marble, Sims, don't be scarce."

With that he vanished.

He could clearly see Marble and Sims. Sure wish I could.

"Thanks all three of you for helping with this," I said. "Now just got to figure out where this big guy belongs."

"Our pleasure, neighbor, Canyon said as I picked up the cat and smiled at the most handsome man.

"If the three of you would ever like to join me," I said, "I have reserved a permanent cabana at the Beach at Mandalay Bay. Great sun and water. That's where I was headed when I discovered our friend here in trouble."

Canyon looked at where I assumed Marble and Sims were, then laughed. "Seems when you arrived we were wondering what to do on a hot summer's day. So if you wouldn't mind, we would love to join you. Give us ten minutes to climb into our suits."

"I'll find this guy's home and be right back."

Then I jumped to my condo, my heart beating with excitement about spending a day with Canyon and two ghost agents.

"So first off what is your name and who is your companion," I asked the big tuxedo cat as I gave him more cold water to drink on my kitchen counter.

I am called Ben. I used to live with my companion named Beth two floors below this condo, but she has died.

"When?" I asked, stunned.

"This morning. I was trying to alert someone when I found myself stuck."

I picked him up and jumped to the dark condo two floors below mine. It was decorated in a heavy Victorian style and smelled a little of lilacs. The blinds were lowered and heavy curtains over them were also pulled closed.

"Is this your place?"

It was, yes, Ben thought at me.

It took only a moment of me yelling for anyone home while I looked through the two-bedroom condo before I found Ben's companion in bed. She was an elderly woman who had clearly died in the middle of the night. Her skin was cold to the touch.

"I am very sorry for your loss," I said to Ben.

She was a good companion.

Carrying Ben, I went back to the front door of the condo and opened it and then left it open a crack. That would be how I got in and how Ben got out in the first place.

Then I jumped back to my condo and called the police and told them what I had found and how I had found the body by trying to return Ben who had escaped. I told them I had Ben in my condo and would be glad to talk with police and give a statement after I got home later in the day.

As a superhero of cats, I often had cats as guests, so I set up a cat box for Ben in my second bathroom, showed him the cat bed, gave him some kibble and some soft food and a large bowl of water, and told him to rest until I got back.

"Looks like you will be staying with me for a time."

I would like that, Ben thought to me.

"But only if you promise to not climb out on a ledge again."

Who said I climbed?

I laughed. It had been a while since I had had a companion in my life and I realized at that moment I was going to enjoy having Ben with me.

Then, right at ten minutes, I jumped to a spot in front of Canyon's door and rang the bell.

And once again Canyon's smile melted me as he opened the door.

And his bare, muscled chest didn't hurt in the slightest.

A good reward for rescuing a cat in my opinion. All in all, it looked like a great day ahead.

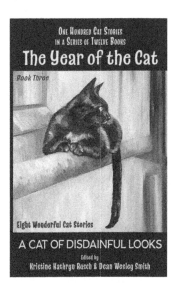

The Year of the Cat Collections
Don't Miss Any of the Twelve

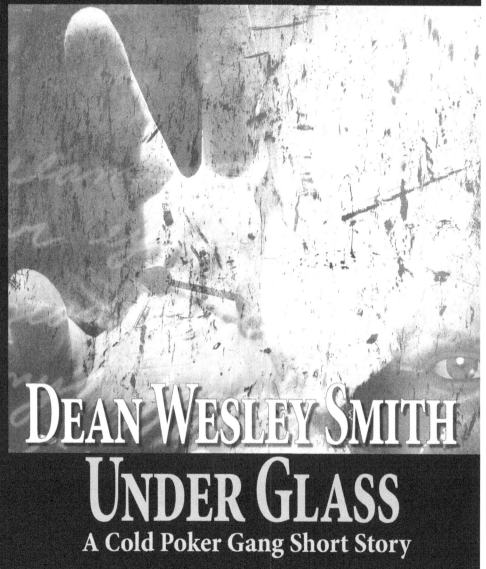

Smith's STORIES

Dean Wesley Smith

Under Glass

A Cold Poker Gang Short Story

A woman's hand, perfectly encased in a box of glass. Found by kids in a field ten years before.

Retired Detectives on the Cold Poker Gang Task Force in Las Vegas finally get assigned the case.

What happened the decade before to the unknown woman?

A twisted Cold Poker Gang mystery short story.

UNDER GLASS
A Cold Poker Gang Story

ONE

RETIRED DETECTIVE Debra Pickett stood staring at the glass box with the woman's hand inside. One of the most famous and stupid cold case files there ever was in the history of Las Vegas. And that was going some.

Around her the sounds of the Las Vegas Police evidence storage area were muffled. The high rows of metal shelves stuffed with file boxes, all carefully marked, really cut down on the sound.

This area was the size of a large gym, only with very low ceilings. They were a good five floors underground here, and Pickett knew the storage went down for more floors and up for more floors. Lots of evidence that never got tossed for one reason or another.

The place had a bad musty odor that Sarge said he never noticed. Retired Detective Ben "Sarge" Carson stood beside her staring at the hand encased in glass.

So far neither of them had said anything.

It was one of those things that either caused jokes or silence.

The hand looked like it had been cut off just yesterday. Clearly the sealed glass box had kept it preserved completely.

It was a woman's hand, left hand, with a large diamond wedding ring on the correct finger. Whoever this hand had belonged to had been rich, or her husband had been. The diamond was very much real and valued back when this was found at over twenty thousand.

Sarge dug into the banker box they had taken the hand in glass out of and pulled out a thin file of reports about the hand. Pickett was sure it would be the same information that they already knew when Andor had assigned them this case.

They had the fingerprints from the hand by photo. And the prints hadn't been in the system. Tests without breaking the glass had proven the hand was real, as was the diamond. It had been found by kids in a field ten years before.

From what experts could tell, again without breaking the perfect glass box, was that the woman had been in her early thirties, was white, and had been regular size in weight, and more than likely had stood between five-six and five-eight.

No record of a woman losing her hand had been found and no missing person's case fit the description.

The case had gotten some laughs around the station, Pickett remembered that. Tough not to make hand jokes with something like this.

Then the case had gone cold.

Now ten long years cold.

She and Sarge and Retired Detective Robin Sprague, their third partner on the cold case task force, were now stuck with this hand, jokes and all. Pickett doubted they would make much headway with this one.

"I don't see here why they didn't crack this open?" Sarge asked.

Sarge had been in a different station when this came in, so he hadn't seen it the first time around like she and Robin had.

"The fine folks in the morgue decided that they would get no more evidence from it by breaking it open."

Pickett picked up the heavy cube with the hand in it and turned it slightly to show Sarge a tiny scar on the lower side of the glass.

"The techs used a tiny drill to get a sample of the air in the box and the DNA from the hand, all without disturbing anything or unsealing it. No need to crack it."

"The DNA was not in the system I assume?" Sarge asked.

"Nothing in the system back then," Pickett said, "but Robin is checking now and looking for familiar matches as well, something that wasn't that common or easy to do when this was found. However, they did find traces of embalming fluid, so the hand, maybe the body before it was cut off, was embalmed."

Pickett, with the heavy glass box in her hands, studied it. The edges where the glass came together were seamless and smooth. Amazing the heat it took to do this kind of glass work didn't destroy the hand inside. This was a master who had created this.

"We need to track down who could do this level of work with glass," Pickett said.

"This sort of screams 'angry husband'," Sarge said.

Pickett had to agree with that.

So with one last look at the glass cube and the severed hand, they put it back in the box, put the box back among the hundreds of thousands of other boxes, and headed back to the clear Las Vegas air.

Pickett would be very thankful to get out of this room full of the evidence of so many crimes. It always gave her the creeps and this time had been no exception.

TWO

PICKETT AND SARGE sat in her Jeep Grand Cherokee and looked through the file even more. There had been a list of glass shops in the original file the detectives had visited. All of them checked out.

Pickett couldn't see a reason to try to go back to the ones still open at this point. That seemed like a dead end.

And besides, an expert said that the glass box, while impressive, could have been made by almost anyone with some basic skills of combining glass over flame.

So at this point, unless Robin came up with something on the DNA search, they were at a complete stop. So Pickett called her and put her on speaker phone.

Pickett and Robin had been partners and best friends when they were both active detectives. They still were partners, even though Sarge had joined the team.

"Find anything new?" Robin asked instead of saying hello.

"Nothing at all," Pickett said.

Sarge, who was sitting in the passenger seat just nodded.

"And no hand jokes?" Robin asked.

"I refrained," Sarge said.

"He did," Pickett said, laughing. "I was very proud of him."

Robin laughed, then said, "Well, I got a hit on the DNA. Looks like a close family member, like a sister. Had sent out for a kidney match five years ago."

"She still alive?" Pickett asked.

"She is," Robin said. "Name is Becky LaMont. She's a hairdresser but isn't working today. Sending the address to your phone. She has a condo near the University."

"Call you when we get done talking with her," Pickett said.

"Great work," Sarge said before Pickett hung up.

Fifteen minutes later they were parked facing a two-story condo complex that seemed to sprawl around a large park-like area. One of the older condo complexes that was for sure. It was ready for another coat of paint, actually.

They knocked and introduced themselves to Becky. She was a thin woman, very short, and more than likely a chain smoker, from the waves of smoke wafting from her apartment. She had big, beach-blonde hair and Pickett almost giggled at how Becky fit right into the stereotype of a low-class hairdresser.

No chance in hell Pickett wanted to be asked into that condo. She might have to burn her clothes afterwards because there was no doubt that smell would never come out.

"Did you happen to have a sister or relative who went missing about ten years ago?" Sarge asked, staying firmly planted right where he was outside the door.

Becky shook her head. "Nope, all my family is accounted for. I wish a few of them would go missing, if you catch my drift. Annoying ain't the word for them."

Pickett nodded. "Did you have a sister or close relative die about ten years ago?"

"Doris," Becky said, nodding and getting a very sad look on her face. "My younger sister. She was the best of us, married some rich guy, then up and died of cancer. Real sad. Tore me up something awful, let me tell you."

Pickett glanced at Sarge. Maybe, just maybe, they might have a lead on the woman's name who had once been attached to the hand.

"Could you give us your sister's name and also her husband's name?" Sarge asked.

Becky did, including where the husband worked, while also spending a few minutes telling them about all the good stuff her sister Doris had done and how much she had helped Becky when times got tough and Becky's second husband beat on her.

Sarge was the one that finally got them away from that door. Becky really was a natural hairdresser. She could keep a client engaged and talking on just about anything.

Pickett had her phone out and was calling Robin with the information before they reached the car.

"It's only eleven," Sarge said as Pickett started the car. "Shall we try his office?"

"Sounds like as good a plan as any."

The guy they were headed to see was Stan Knott, an attorney. Robin got back to them with even more information about Knott. He was well-respected, did a lot of charity work, and had never remarried after his wife and childhood sweetheart, Doris Knott, died of aggressive lung cancer.

His offices were comfortable, desert art and brown tones. When Pickett and Sarge showed the secretary their badges, they got right in to see Stan.

Stan had on a silk dress shirt, his tie off and collar open, and his silk jacket hanging on an antique coat tree in one corner.

The office had a huge desk, slightly cluttered, two chairs in front of the desk, and a couch and chair against one wall facing a large screen in the corner.

There was a framed picture of Stan and an attractive woman on the wall behind Stan with some of his degrees.

"Is that your wife Doris?" Pickett asked, pointing at the picture after they introduced themselves.

"It is," Stan said, pointing that they should take a seat. "So what can I help you with?"

"We think we found Doris's hand with a wedding ring on it," Sarge said. "Sealed in a glass cube."

"Is this some sort of joke?" Stan asked, his voice low and controlled, but clearly angry. "Because if it is, it is certainly not funny."

Pickett took a photo of the hand out of her purse. "This was found by kids playing in a field ten years ago now."

She slid the picture to Stan who stared at it and then slowly seemed to stop breathing.

He stood and moved over to the photo on the wall and took it down, bringing it to Pickett.

She looked at the photo. Doris's left hand was clearly visible and it sure looked like the same shape and the same ring.

"Did you bury your wife with her wedding ring?" Sarge asked.

"I did," Stan said, his voice soft.

Pickett took the photo back and gave him back his framed picture.

"This is how you remember your wife," Pickett said, pointing at the framed picture of the smiling couple. "We'll figure out what happened here."

Stan nodded.

"Do we have your permission to exhume your wife to double check and find evidence of what might have happened?"

Stan sat there for a moment, silent, then he said simply, "Of course."

Pickett couldn't even image what he was going through.

THREE

THEY HAD CONVINCED Stan that he didn't need to be at the grave and didn't want to be. So besides the crew doing the work, Pickett and Sarge and Robin stood off to one side as they lifted the casket out of the ground.

The cemetery was one of the expensive ones in the valley, with real trees, mostly oak, and some palm trees along one side. The grass was freshly mowed and smelled wonderful in the warm fall day.

The morning sun was just starting to crest the distant mountains and the dew on the grass from the sprinklers was still holding on.

Once the casket was settled on a wooden platform beside the grave, the workers unlocked it and opened both halves.

"Shit," one of the workers said, stepping back and then turning away.

The other worker just stared for a moment before stepping back as well.

Pickett and Robin and Sarge moved across the grass so that they could see why seasoned cemetery workers had had a reaction like that.

It took a moment for Pickett to completely understand exactly what she was seeing.

There looked to be a woman's body in the casket, but the woman had no hands, no feet, and no head. Her dress had been torn open and both her breasts had been removed and her crotch had been cut out.

Pickett wanted to be sick. In all her years, she had never seen anything like this level of mutilation of a body.

Sarge turned to the workers. "Close this up and call the station. We'll fill in the active detective who is going to take this one over."

Pickett knew that was the end of this case for them.

With that, Sarge and Robin and Pickett turned away, heading back to their cars.

Pickett was glad for that. She sure didn't need to see any more.

And she really felt bad for Stan who still hadn't gotten over losing the love of his life. This was going to be very difficult to deal with.

"We did what we set out to do," Robin said as they got to their cars. "We solved the cold case of the hand in the box."

"And now we are off the case," Pickett said. "This just went active faster than anything I have seen before. And honestly, can't say I am unhappy with that."

"Neither am I," Robin said.

"I will agree to that completely," Sarge said. "I don't ever want to meet the sick-o who could do that to a woman's body."

"Or even try to imagine the reason," Robin said.

Suddenly Pickett had an idea. Someone had to have a reason and that kind of mutilation looked angry.

"Robin, before we go turning this over to the active side completely, could you look up a few things."

The morning so nice, the air so crisp, that Robin nodded and set up her laptop on the hood of Pickett's car.

"So what do you want?"

"Who was Becky, Doris's sister married to ten years ago?"

Sarge was looking at her with a puzzled look, so while Robin did a quick search, Pickett explained to Sarge and Robin her wild thought.

Becky had said that her husband at the time had been beating her and Doris stepped in and helped. That had to be a motive for some really deep hate.

"His name was Tom Davis," Robin said. "He's serving time right now in the state prison for two counts of double murder because he got angry and beat two women to death."

"Becky was lucky to get out alive," Sarge said.

"You're not kidding," Pickett said.

"Oh, my," Robin said, shaking her head. "Look where he worked during that time."

She turned the laptop around so that Pickett and Sarge could both see it. It seemed that good old violent Tom had worked at a glass-forming plant that made special windows and glass fixtures for hotels and casinos. He could have easily shaped that box with the hand in it.

"Seems we just gave the new active detective on this case a helping hand," Sarge said.

Pickett looked up at him sternly as he pretended to be innocent. "You were doing so well."

"He was," Robin said. "You got to hand it to him."

Pickett turned to her best friend who also pretended to just work on shutting down her laptop.

Then Pickett laughed and all three of them laughed.

After seeing what they had just seen and solving the case, a few jokes were required.

They were all headed for breakfast and they would be sorry they started this because she had a handful of her own.

~

More WMG Writer's Guides

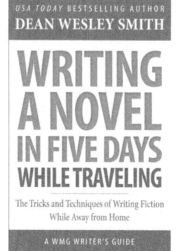

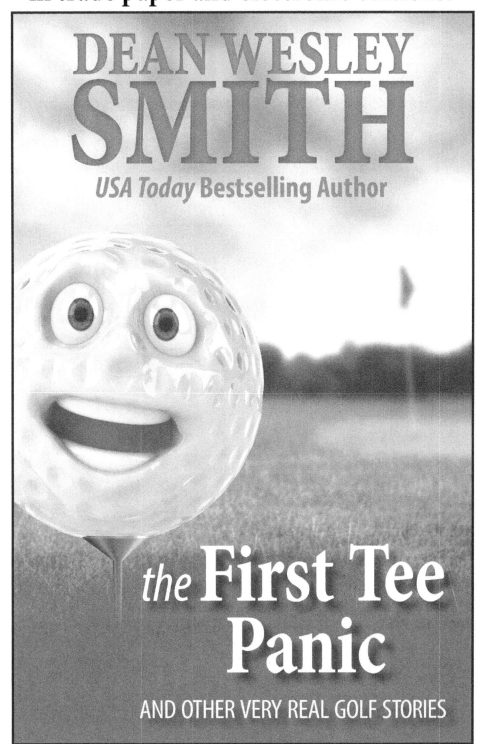

Smith's
STORIES

DEAN WESLEY SMITH
USA Today Bestselling Writer

A MENU OF MEMORY
A Bryant Street Short Story

Every day J.C. Dunn comes home to his wonderful house on Bryant Street. He used to love the place, now he fears it. Every night it smells of spaghetti sauce and fresh garlic bread.

He lives by himself and never cooks anything like that. But the smell, every day, persists, like a swarm of insects invading his home.

I wrote this story in honor of my departed good friend Kip. When I started off writing, I worked for him in his spaghetti restaurant. A magical place.

Later on, until he died, he hosted writer workshops that Kris and I taught in his remodeled hotel. I still miss him.

A MENU OF MEMORY
A Bryant Street Story

J.C. DUNN UNLOCKED the large wooden front door to his standard ranch house in the subdivision of Bryant Street and just stood there, afraid of what he might find if he pushed that door open.

For years, he had loved to come home to what he called his "retreat in the city." Now, he had come to dread it. The house was starting to drive him slowly crazy.

J.C. was a short man, not more than five-one at best, and he always wore his best suits to work and never took off his jacket. Today was no exception, even though the early fall day was warm and the sun still fairly hot. Normally, once he got inside, he allowed himself to put on comfortable brown cotton slacks, dark brown slippers, and an older dress shirt that he rolled the sleeves up.

He loved that routine. Now he feared it.

He carefully pushed the large door open. The air from the inside hit him squarely in the face. Once again the house smelled of spaghetti sauce. Onion, garlic, green peppers all blended together in a tomato-based mixture. And behind that was the rich, thick smell of fresh garlic bread, like it had just come out of the oven.

The damned smell almost felt hot, it was so real.

Only problem, J.C. Dunn hadn't cooked spaghetti in his thirty years of living in this house. And he had lived here by himself the entire time. And up until just a week ago, the house had smelled normal, like his lilac-scented dryer sheets or the turkey TV dinner he had just heated up. But more often it smelled faintly of old books that he had filled shelves with. And old photos in antique and ornate wood frames he had covered a number of walls with.

He loved that smell, felt comfortable living surrounded by that.

He called all the faces in the old photos his adopted family, even though he didn't know any of them. He had never had a real family, so why not have antique photos of people he could call family.

And often he loved the art of the old carved frames far more than the pictures they contained.

That faint musty odor he loved, but never spaghetti or garlic bread. He wouldn't have a clue how to even start to cook either one.

But for seemingly forever now that garlic and fresh bread smell had invaded his house like a swarm of ants that he couldn't figure out how to kill.

And he had tried.

One day he left all the doors and windows open during the evening. Smell didn't go away in the slightest. He tried air-freshener, but that just created a nasty smell that once again he had to open doors and windows to clear just to get back to the spaghetti smell.

The garlic bread and spaghetti odor didn't seem to be coming from anywhere exactly in the house, yet it was extremely strong and never dissipated. Eating his morning oatmeal over the old-fashioned print newspaper had been ruined. His oatmeal had started tasting like garlic bread, so much so that for the first time in years, he had had to go out for breakfast.

Now his co-workers down at Anderson and Peters Accounting were starting to mention how he smelled like fresh garlic bread. They called it wonderful and said it made them hungry. That has scared him even more because he had almost convinced himself he was imagining the smell.

If others could smell it, it wasn't his imagination.

Something very real was happening and he needed to find out what before he had to leave his wonderful "retreat in the city."

J.C. closed the door behind him and feeling like he was wading through the air, he went and changed clothes. Then he almost swam back to the kitchen to start to cook himself a TV dinner. He had to eat, even if the turkey tasted like garlic.

As he stood there at his Formica kitchen counter, sipping on a glass of white wine, he took out a note pad and tried to write down the first time he smelled spaghetti and garlic bread in the house.

It had been Sunday morning just four days ago.

Four days going on an eternity.

So what had he done Saturday night? Nothing but his normal reading of an antique Zane Gray novel in original hardback with dust jacket.

So what had he done during the day last Saturday? He had had his normal breakfast, then did a little work he had brought home from the office, then made himself a sandwich and put it and a banana in a paper bag and went to the Seventh Street Auction.

He loved auctions, even though he seldom bought anything. He liked being around the people and watching the value of things he remembered as a kid go for stupidly high prices.

And every so often a box of old books would come up for sale and he would bid on them, never going very high. He would maybe keep one or two for his own collection and give the rest away. He was very selective as to what he kept. He was afraid of being a hoarder instead of a collector. He liked his house neat and clean and everything in its place, like a good set of accounting ledgers.

He went to three different auctions a month. It was his one real form of entertainment out of the house.

So what had happened last Saturday at that auction? Now he remembered. He had bought a box of old framed photos. He had put them in his second bedroom until he got a chance to look at them. Could it be one of those framed photos causing the issue?

He didn't see how, but at this point, just short of going completely crazy, he was going to check everything.

He shut off the microwave and let his dinner sit, then headed down the hall to the second bedroom. The house had three bedrooms. His master bedroom, a guest room he kept clean for a guest, which

in all the years he had lived here he had never had, and then his third bedroom that he used for his auction hobby.

The door was closed to his third bedroom, as he normally kept it, and inside the small bedroom it smelled the same as the rest of the house.

He had a desk on one wall with a computer on it he used to look up prices of things on eBay and details about a book or picture he had found.

He had a long folding table against a wall that he used to sort the few things he bought at an auction, deciding what would go to a local charity and what little bit he would keep. He had put the cardboard box of framed photos on the table and hadn't even looked at them since he had been so distracted by the smell.

He had gotten the entire box for ten dollars and the auctioneer said it had come from an estate.

The smell wasn't any worse around the box, but it wasn't any better either.

The first framed picture he took out was of a woman standing beside a horse somewhere on a ranch. It looked to be from around 1920 and she had a nice smile on her face. And the frame almost looked hand-carved and polished. He might keep that one.

The next two pictures were standard family shots of large groups and he set those aside to give away.

The next frame held a menu.

It was printed on what looked like cheap paper and the frame was cheap. The menu was stained with some red sauce, or at least J.C. hoped it was a red sauce and not blood.

The menu was for a place called Kip's Spaghetti Restaurant.

J.C. was stunned. A full spaghetti dinner, plus salad and garlic bread was only

99 cents back then. If he had to guess, it was from the late 1970s or early 1980s.

He looked at the back of the frame. Nothing written there.

He didn't know how it was happening, but he had gotten this framed menu of a spaghetti restaurant on Saturday and starting Sunday his house smelled like a spaghetti restaurant.

Not possible, just not possible.

But neither was a smell hanging around like this. Over the years he had gotten some musty, moldy books that smelled up the house and he had had to take them out and throw them away.

But this was different. Very different.

He held the frame up and looked at it, then decided the best thing to do with it was put it in the trunk of his car to see if that actually helped anything. His logical numbers brain didn't think it would, but he was getting desperate.

J.C. walked the framed menu out to his car, put it in the trunk and went back inside. No one was out in the early evening along the tree-lined street.

By the time he got back inside, the smell had gotten noticeably less, so he opened the windows and doors and within a half hour most of the place smelled almost back to normal. He would have to wash all the sheets and have his suits cleaned and do a ton of loads of washing to get the smell out of everything, but at least he had found the problem.

But he had no idea how an old menu could be so powerful, almost magical in its smell.

He had no idea what to do with it either. No doubt tomorrow his car would smell like garlic bread, but that, for the moment, was a lot better than his entire house.

That evening he started a few loads of laundry so he would have clean shirts and underwear tomorrow and hung one of his suits out to air on the back porch to get as much of the smell out of it as he could.

The next morning his oatmeal once again tasted like oatmeal and he could just barely smell the garlic bread on his clothes.

But he was right, his car smelled just as his house had smelled for four days.

He opened the car windows all the way around to air it out some, then went back into his house and to his computer after calling work to say he would be in at noon today, something he had never done before.

But he had to do something with the menu, and for some reason he couldn't bring himself to throw it away.

Online he found three different Italian restaurants within easy drive of Bryant Street. He took down their addresses and got in the car, driving with the air conditioning running and the windows open to keep the smell down as much as he could.

The first restaurant hadn't opened yet, so he headed to the next one. There he found the owner after a few knocks on the door. The guy did not invite him in and J.C. was glad for that, to be honest. He had smelled enough Italian food to last a lifetime.

The manager was an older, heavyset guy, about sixty or so, with white hair and large eyebrows. He had to be a ways over six foot tall, so he towered over J.C. but J.C. was used to people doing that.

The guy wore jeans, a too-small T-shirt, and a red-stained apron.

"Hi," J.C. said and introduced himself, standing in the warming sun just in front of the restaurant's door. The owner just stood in the open door and nodded, not bothering to introduce himself.

Clearly he expected J.C. to try to sell him something.

"At the auction on Saturday," J.C. said, "I found an old, framed menu of a spaghetti house that I think was around here somewhere."

The manager nodded.

"It's for a place called 'Kip's Spaghetti Restaurant' and it sold spaghetti dinners for only 99 cents."

"You found an old menu from Kip's?" the guy asked, now clearly interested. "My parents and I used to go there all the time. It was magical."

J.C. nodded to that. "I have experienced that. So I am wondering if you would like the menu, no cost. It was in a box of old pictures I bought and I just want to get it to a good home."

Suddenly the big man had a smile on his face that made him look like a kid. "I would love that."

"Let me get it," J.C. said, heading quickly to his car and popping the trunk.

He grabbed the framed menu and handed it to the owner who just beamed looking at it.

"Damn, does this bring back memories. I can almost smell the place. And the spaghetti sauce was so good and the slice of garlic bread was to die for. I've owned this place for twenty years and I still don't know how Kip did that, let alone sold entire dinners for 99 cents."

"Magic," J.C. said.

"I think it might have been," the manager said, nodding and staring at the menu. He reached out and shook J.C.'s hand, then said, "Thank you."

"I'm just glad it got a good home," J.C. said.

"A great home," the manager said. "Come on in some night. Dinner is on me."

"Thank you," J.C. said. "I just might."

He had no intention of going near this place and that menu again.

Not ever.

J.C. liked his life structured, his books old, and his family made up in antique frames on his wall. He had no time for magic of any sort.

The smell was mostly gone from his car by the time he got to work. And no one said he smelled like garlic bread the entire day.

That night he could actually taste his turkey TV dinner. Life was wonderful on Bryant Street once again.

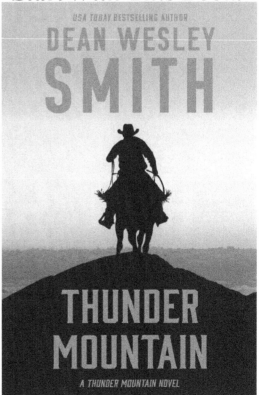

USA TODAY BESTSELLING AUTHOR

DEAN WESLEY SMITH

HOT SPRINGS MEADOW

A THUNDER MOUNTAIN NOVEL

Jenny Lind, a traveler from the institute, found back in 1902 a hidden hot springs near the boomtown of Roosevelt.

In 2018, traveler Kathryn "Flag" Sinclair found an article that Jenny wrote for a local paper in 1903 about the hidden hot springs. And went in search of the hot springs.

Neither woman knew the other, or knew the other was a traveler from the institute back in time.

What happens next spans more than a century and might be one of the more twisted Thunder Mountain novels yet.

HOT SPRINGS MEADOW
A Thunder Mountain Short Novel

PART ONE
A Meet Naked

ONE

June 26th, 1902
Monumental Creek, Central Idaho

JENNY LINDE let the hot sun that hit the bottom of the deep canyon warm her like a soft blanket, but only a moment. Sun in these mountains was to be treasured. Then she nudged her horse Constance into the shade of the pine trees towering around her and started up the narrow side canyon. It felt like it had been days since she had actually been warm through and through.

The Idaho wilderness in early summer had temperatures that could vary from bitterly cold at night to dry and hot during the day. But in June in the steep canyons of the Monumental Creek drainage, the sun seldom got to the canyon floor and the air rarely warmed up. However in July and August that was another story. Those were the hot months at this high altitude.

The smell of warm pine needles filled the thin air as she started to climb up the narrow canyon. To her, that smell promised summer and reminded her of all the camping trips with her parents. Fun memories, even though now they seemed very distant through the hundreds of years she had already lived.

Patches of snow, some white, some dirty brown, still covered the ground under trees and along the stream. Most of the runoff from the snowmelt in this area had subsided, leaving this stream running just slightly higher than normal and a few degrees louder as well. If it hadn't subsided, she never would have been able to get into this narrow canyon at all.

After just a few minutes, she dismounted because the climb was too steep and rough, with too much brush and overhanging branches. Then for the next thirty minutes, like working her way up a never-ending flight of stairs, she led her gray and white mare along the very narrow, steep-walled side canyon, the entire time wondering why in the world she was spending the time on such a crazy idea.

She had to carefully pick her way over the rocks and through the brush. She finally gave up trying to stay dry and led Constance slowly up the middle of the stream. After thirty minutes, that exercise alone had her too warm while her legs were numb from the cold water. Climbing against rushing water was never easy.

She stopped and just stood in the middle of the rushing stream, the cold water swirling around her boots made her lower legs almost feel like stumps. She let Constance drink, watching her for a moment. Jenny didn't dare spend much more time in the water before taking a break.

She splashed her face with the cold creek water. That felt heavenly, like a great shot of tequila. Quality tequila. She seldom drank anything while living back in the past. Nothing here worth drinking to be honest.

But when home in 2021, a great shot of tequila sometimes was just what the doctor ordered. And since she had a couple doctorates in history and journalism, she figured she could prescribe anything she wanted for herself.

Let's test this again," she said aloud to Constance. Her voice didn't make it past the rushing water sounds of the stream around her as it echoed off the steep rocks and pines towering over her.

Constance just ignored her and kept drinking.

Jenny moved to a hidden pocket in her saddlebag and pulled out a thin instrument that looked exactly like an old slide rule of this time period, but was actually something far more sophisticated. She had brought it with her from 2021. She knew that such things, by Institute rules, weren't allowed in the past, but she had promised Director Parks to be careful with it and he had surprisingly agreed. He had laughed and said he liked her reasons for wanting to take it.

She used the instrument to take a quick sample of the water and could see that the sulfur content was actually slightly higher than it had been near where this stream flowed into Monumental Creek. The device also tested for a dozen other minerals and contaminates and clearly this water had a decent concentration of minerals.

She hadn't been able to taste the sulfur at all in the water. It just tasted pure and cold and clear.

She put the instrument back and patted Constance. "We haven't passed the hot springs yet."

She wasn't sure if that was good or bad. She just really wanted to find a hot springs that she could soak in for a time. Traveling in the Idaho wilderness was never an easy thing, so finding hot springs had been her hobby the last five or six times back into the past.

And this stream was the only one along Monumental Creek, from where it ran into Big Creek, that had shown any signs at all of a possible hot springs. But looking ahead, the climb up this canyon clearly wasn't going to get easier.

She eased Constance forward and for the next twenty minutes they carefully worked their way over the rocks and through the water, mostly just using the stream bed as a trail, since there was no room on the canyon walls on either

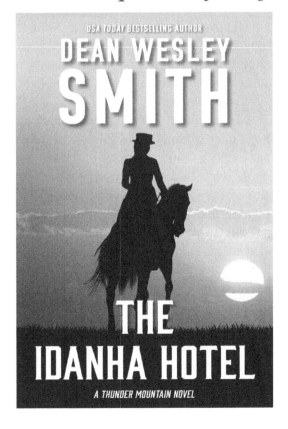
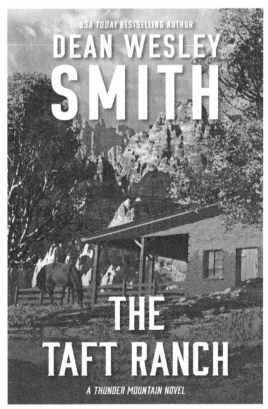

side. She had been in wider hallways at Stanford than the bottom of this canyon.

Finally, the rock walls opened slightly. It didn't take much to feel open compared to what felt like a narrow flight of stairs they had been going up.

The watermarks on the rocks around her showed that this area at the peak time for the snowmelt would fill with water. The hallway-sized area they had just come through clearly worked as a choke point.

Luckily, at the moment, the area had drained and was wide enough and with no brush so that it would be possible to ride again.

Jenny led Constance out of the water and mounted up, moving slowly forward along the scoured rock next to the stream.

Only twice in the next ten minutes did they have to go back into the water.

Then, almost like a curtain parting, they came through a small stand of pine trees and into a fairly flat and large meadow, bathed in sunlight and covered in bright green grass.

"Wow," Jenny said, stopping and just staring at the sight in front of her.

The rock mountain walls went up into the blue sky on all sides of the meadow, making it feel like she was in a protected bottom of a beautiful brown bowl.

The sun filled the entire small valley, making everything seem brighter.

The stream sort of meandered through the meadow, like a painting you might see on a hotel room wall. And the colors were so bright, they felt almost artificial. The greens of the fresh grass, the blues of the bright sky, the browns of the rock walls, the dark shapes of the pine trees against the rocks. Everything was so bright and stark, it was difficult to take in.

"We may have just climbed up into heaven," Jenny said, patting Constance on the neck.

And then Jenny laughed and the sound carried through the open meadow like a glass wind chime moving in a gentle breeze.

TWO

November 17th, 2018
Boise, Idaho

KATHRYN "FLAG" SINCLAIR sat back in her black leather office chair and smiled at her computer screen. She had just found something worth looking into that might change a few geological theories of the mountains of the Central Idaho Wilderness.

Flag was at her mahogany desk in her personal office in the main library of the Historical Institute in Boise, Idaho. The desk and chair had had to be custom made for her because on a good day she stood five-foot-three, and that counted her cowboy boots.

At thirty-two, she still ate as much as she wanted and managed to stay rail thin, just like her mother and her grandmother before her. She kept her light-brown hair cut short which made her face look even rounder, and her bright green eyes made her look at times like a large doll head on a stick figure.

She didn't care. And she didn't care in the slightest that she always wore the same thing. Jeans with cowboy boots, a sports bra even though she really didn't need a bra, and a light dress blouse.

And she wore no rings or jewelry. Nothing. Just too damn much trouble to bother with.

Her one vice, besides being completely focused on her work as a specialist in geological near-time history, was a good margarita. Two bars in Boise made top-flight margaritas, and when home here in 2018, she spent numbers of evenings in one or the other, drinking and doing some two-step dancing.

She stood and paced for a moment. She had more than enough room to pace, something she loved about this office. It was big enough so that it not only held her custom-made desk, but a large dark cloth couch, a reading recliner that also fit her perfectly, and two walls of bookshelves.

One shelf of one bookcase held copies of the five published books that she had written on near-time geological history and its impact on the miners and settlers in the Pacific Northwest.

The article she had just found was about a hot springs in a meadow just off of Monumental Creek. It had been written in 1903 by a Jenny Linde and published in a small-town Idaho newspaper.

Lind had given the location of the hot springs and the meadow as between where Monumental Creek dumped into Big Creek and the boomtown of Roosevelt. She said nothing more about the location, as if trying to keep it a secret. The distance she talked about in the article was almost thirty miles with more side creeks than Flag wanted to think about.

But this Jenny Linde had named the place Hot Springs Meadow, as if it was very, very real.

And that meant that if Jenny Linde hadn't been making up the entire thing, there was a hot springs where there shouldn't be a hot springs.

Flag knew that fact because hot springs were the topic of her next book. She didn't have a title yet, but her tag line was: *Hot springs and their impact and use by Native Americans and early settlers.*

Now the Central Idaho Mountains had numbers of hot springs, actually up in the thousands, but not in that area Jenny Linde wrote about. It was believed that the structure of the mountains there just wouldn't allow them. Flag had doubted that theory for a very long time, and now, just maybe she had some proof.

She spent another hour doing more research, including starting to study satellite photos of the area, looking for a meadow of any kind. Then she headed out for dinner and a celebration.

By the time the night was over, she had had one too many margaritas in celebration and had to take an Uber back to her Institute condo instead of walking like she normally did.

Still, a fun evening after a fun discovery.

By the next morning at ten she was recovered and for the next three days and much of the nights, she kept up her research.

She found, in the process, two more references to Hot Springs Meadow located in the same area off of Monumental Creek.

The meadow didn't show up on any map, but that wasn't going to stop her. She would find it if it took ten years. In the past, she had the time.

More than enough time, actually.

THREE

June 26th, 1902
Hot Springs Meadow, Central Idaho

JENNY TRACED the sulfur and mineral-tainted water in the stream up to a small side stream of water near the top of the meadow coming down from some large rocks.

She followed that small stream up the hill until she found the source of the sulfur. Hot thermal water bubbled from between two boulders. The smell of sulfur was faint, but clear right at the source, as it sometimes was near the point hot water came out of the ground. Moss covered some of the rocks around the stream's origin and the entire area felt slick and slightly slimy.

Jenny went back down through the rocks to a point about twenty feet below the spring and felt the water temperature of the flow. Perfect. And around her were enough rocks she could move to make a great dam to form a pool of hot water.

"Need some food and a camp before I start this," she said to herself, heading back to where she had left Constance grazing on the green spring grass.

After a short search, she found a perfect campsite, flat for her tent, good shelter for the fire, and some rocks easy to move to sit on. And it was just about thirty paces below where she planned on building the hot water pool.

Then she got Constance unsaddled, brushed, and settled in.

"We're going to be here a few days, girl," Jenny said. "Enjoy it. I know I will."

In fact, Jenny didn't need to be into the mining boomtown of Roosevelt for almost two weeks. She wanted to be there when the newspaper was getting started and work for it. No better way to study the newspapers of the west than go around working for them as they got started. So that gave her at least a week in this beautiful place, maybe even a little more.

Jenny made sure Constance was comfortable, had enough to eat and water, then patted her neck again. Damn, Jenny loved that horse. In all her times back into the past, she had always tried to get Constance from the Institute stable. The two of them just sort of fit together. And in all the trips, she had only lost Constance to accidents twice. Both times it had torn her up more than she wanted to admit.

Jenny then explored the small valley on foot.

It looked to be the size of a football stadium. The rock walls and pine trees above made the place into a perfect bowl and the sun filled the valley for longer than most valleys in this area of mountains got sun.

There were a few animal trails, clearly made by deer. She saw no other signs of anything else.

Some patches of snow still covered parts of one side of the valley and she was very relieved to see no snakes at all. This was just too cold and too high on the mountain for them.

She also saw not one sign of any human ever being up here before. No prospector, no Native American, no one. She might very well be the first in this fantastic little valley. And that both excited her and terrified her.

If she hadn't spent so many decades in the past in these mountains, mostly alone, she never would be able to stay in a place like this.

Now, to her, this felt safe.

And perfect.

FOUR

November 20th, 2018
Boise, Idaho

FLAG WALKED from the Institute's modern-looking library building where her office was and up the tree-lined trail beside the Boise River to the main Institute building. The day was cold with a gray overcast that threatened nothing but depression. She had put on a light jacket and stocking cap and gloves for the walk. The river below the winding bike trail was running low and dark gray, matching the mood of the sky.

She still loved the walk, the bite of the air on her cheeks and the time mostly alone to gather her thoughts.

The walk took ten minutes before she approached the main office of the Institute. The building was a perfectly kept Victorian mansion on a large estate above the river. Stately Oak and Willow trees surrounded the mansion, their leaves now long gone and swept away by the fall winds.

The building, maintained to look exactly like it had looked when built in the 1880s, always impressed visitors. It had impressed her the first time she saw it and it still did.

But under the mansion was what was really impressive. A massive number of caverns carved out of rock that very, very few people even knew about. Those caverns had been carved back when the mansion was being constructed in the 1880s by out-of-the-area laborers and miners, now all long dead. And back then, this mansion was a long coach ride outside of Boise. Now it felt almost in the middle of the city.

The Institute invited numbers of researchers to Boise and the half-dozen institute buildings to work on various research topics of their own choosing, usually something to do with history or math. The Institute paid the researcher's way, gave them a nice condo on the river to live in, and a large monthly salary that wasn't needed because the Institute provided free food and cars as well.

It was a researcher's dream, and she had felt herself fantastically lucky to be invited.

Then, after a year of working in her wonderful office, getting ready to write her third book, she was approached by Director Parks, a tall, handsome man who she knew was one of the founders. He had invited her to join him and two of the other legendary founders, Duster and Bonnie Kendal. She had never met them before that day, but they were known worldwide for the generosity and their fantastic mathematical minds.

They were even more impressive in person, towering over her like mythical giants. Of course, at five-three, most people towered over her, but Bonnie and Duster felt even larger for some reason.

Then they had showed her the caverns and proven to her that it really was possible to jump back into the past of basically identical timelines.

As far as she knew, right now there were fewer than thirty people traveling into the past from this point in time. Thirty other researchers who knew about these caverns.

That was it.

And what was even more amazing was that while back in the past in another timeline, only two minutes and fifteen seconds elapsed in her present timeline here in 2018.

She could live a full life in the Old West, die of old age there, and only just over two minutes would have passed here in 2018.

That had taken her months to wrap her mind around.

And it seemed the Institute stretched hundreds of years into the future as well.

No one was allowed to move forward without permission, but Director Parks had taken her one hundred years into the future. Then they had come back, which meant that only 2 minutes and 15 seconds of that future time was elapsing in her life now.

And it had only been five months in her 2018 time now, but she had lived over seven hundred years in the past and managed to do the research on and write five more books under her own name and six under other names.

Seven hundred wonderful years of learning and study.

She had died twice, both times of disease. And once lived to almost sixty before coming back to the present.

As the years in the past went by, she slowly came to realize that for all intents, she was immortal. If she got killed walking to the Institute main building right now, she would wake up a hundred years in the future with only a couple minutes gone and just come back again.

And when she grew old and died in this timeline, she could just come back again to basically an identical timeline and just keep living.

She thought she had been lucky before. This was just flat beyond understanding. One day she had been a college professor trying to write a few books in her area of passion in her spare time, the next she was immortal and traveling for hundreds of years in the past.

She walked slowly past the garage that used to be the stables and into the back door of the old mansion. Making sure no one was around, she then keyed a hidden door and went through and down a number of flights of stairs to the main cavern under the mansion. She was right on time for the meeting she had requested with Bonnie and Duster and Director Parks.

Bonnie and Duster knew the Monumental Valley better than anyone. She needed to find out if they knew about Hot Springs Meadow before she went back looking for it.

The huge main cavern was called "The Living Room" because the massive cavern had at least twenty areas of couches and chairs and tables, all set in a way to allow talking in groups. A large river-stone fireplace dominated one wall and it had a small fire in it right now, crackling slightly and giving the cavern a wonderful odor of burning wood. Perfect for this time of the late fall.

Across one wall of the massive cavern was a long kitchen-counter with stools. Flag bet that all the people who traveled in the past from this moment could sit at the same time at that counter, it was that long.

They had built this for a time in the future when there would be a lot more travelers.

Behind the counter was a full and modern kitchen with a number of fridges and stoves. Then off to one side were showers and locker rooms. You had to go through this cavern to get to the caverns below with the supplies for traveling into the past and the rooms full of crystals that allowed it all to happen.

So this big "living room" cavern was the central point for just about anything.

But that said, in all her trips back, she had never run into another traveler in this living room without making an appointment to meet them here.

Duster Kendal sat at the counter, working at a sandwich and a bowl of soup that smelled like chicken noodle. Duster wore his usual long brown leather duster and had his cowboy hat on the stool beside him. Flag had never seen him out of that duster, no matter the weather.

Director Parks sat to his right, also eating. Parks was dressed in a business suit. Clearly he had come down from his office upstairs for lunch and this meeting she had requested.

Bonnie stood against a back counter sipping on some soup. She had on jeans, a silk blouse, and had her long dark hair pulled back. They were the only three in the large cavern, besides her.

And all of these people were giants compared to Flag. Duster and Director Parks had to be over six foot tall and Bonnie was at least five-ten. They just towered over her.

"You want some soup?" Bonnie asked, smiling as she saw Flag working her way through the couches and chairs toward the counter.

"No thanks," Flag said. "Just ate."

And she had back in her office before heading here. A microwave pasta dish that hadn't had much taste at all.

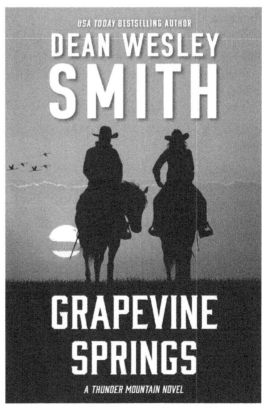

Flag went around behind the counter and took off her coat and hat and gloves and put them on the counter a ways away from both men. Then she poured herself a mug of hot water from the kettle on the stove and made herself some hot chocolate with the small marshmallows and all. It was getting cold enough and besides her morning coffee, hot chocolate was her drink of the winter. She kept a large supply of it here in the cavern and often put a bunch in her pack when she went into the past.

"So, Dr. Sinclair," Duster said, pushing his empty soup bowl aside and pulling what looked like a massive turkey sandwich on white bread closer. "What is this all about?"

"A hot springs," Flag said, ignoring the fact that Duster had addressed her officially. Normally he just called her Flag.

"In a place called Hot Springs Meadow."

"Never heard of it," Bonnie said, shaking her head.

"Where is this supposed to be?" Duster asked.

"Between Roosevelt and Big Creek up a side canyon off of Monumental Creek."

That sentence was the very sentence she wanted to say in front of Bonnie and Duster and Director Parks. It was the entire reason for asking them to be here.

Flag had no idea how old those three were, but she did know it was thousands and thousands of years and many of those years had been spent in that Monumental valley in those mountain.

"Not there," Duster said, not even looking up from his sandwich.

Both Bonnie and Director Parks looked at her with puzzled frowns.

"So why do you think there is a Hot Springs Meadow in that area?" Director Parks asked.

"Three different mentions of it in different newspapers of the time," Flag said. "And I think maybe I might have found it."

"Not anywhere along Monumental," Duster said, still not even looking up from his sandwich while shaking his head. "No hot springs at all in that area."

Flag moved over to her coat and pulled out a thin file she had brought and was going to take with her into the past. It contained a topographic map of the area and also a satellite photo. On both she had circled what she thought was the meadow up almost a half mile on a small, unnamed side creek.

She showed them first to Bonnie, who nodded after a moment and then handed them to Director Parks, who after looking handed them to Duster.

After a moment of study, Duster again just shook his head and pushed the file away. "Tell you what. You find a hot springs along Monumental Creek and I'll buy you a night of those margaritas you love so much."

"How about a steak dinner instead, with one margarita included?" Flag asked, smiling. "And I buy the same for you if I don't find it."

Duster laughed and stuck out his hand.

Flag shook his hand, his engulfing hers.

"Deal," he said.

"It's a bet," she said.

"When you starting the search?" Parks asked.

I'm headed back right now," Flag said.

Duster laughed. "I'll still be right here working on the rest of this sandwich when you come back and tell me where you are going to take me to dinner."

Flag laughed. "I'm really going to savor that steak."

Bonnie and Parks both laughed.

Then Bonnie said, "You find a hot springs along that Monumental trail and trust me, it will be worth a steak or two. Can't tell you how many times traveling that trail I could have used one."

Duster just nodded to that and kept eating.

FIVE

June 27th, 1902
Hot Springs Meadow, Central Idaho

JENNY SPENT the rest of the afternoon of her first day in the small bowl-shaped valley building her camp, gathering firewood and then cooking herself a nice dinner of beef stew and potatoes she had carried with her up from Cascade. It felt like time to celebrate a little, since she had found what she had been looking for.

She then spent part of the late afternoon seeing if there were trout living in the deep pockets of the stream as it wandered through the meadow. There were, and she managed to catch two for tomorrow's meals before the bugs coming out as the sun went behind the mountains drove her back to the campfire.

She loved the smell of a burning campfire and just sitting near one and watching the stars come out in the evening. There was just nothing better.

She turned in early and the first rays of the sun clipping the tops of the mountains above her woke her. That climb up that creek bed to find this valley had left

her with a few sore muscles, but not as many as she had feared.

She got the fire built back up and water boiling for some hot tea, then checked on Constance and got her fed and brushed before going back to the fire to wrap up and cook one of the nice trout she had caught last night.

She didn't often manage fresh trout for breakfast, but when she did, there was nothing better, especially baked in breadcrumbs with butter and wrapped up tight in foil. The light meat just fell off the bones.

By the time the first rays of light started to hit the valley floor, she had on her work gloves and had her folding shovel in her hand. She was ready to build a hot springs pool.

She first cleared the rocks out of an area about the size of a decent hot tub, leaving only dirt and sand and a few flat rocks with the small stream going through it.

Then working on first the left, then the right, she managed to move larger rocks into place. There was a pretty decent amount of hot water running down from the spring above her, but she was still going to have to make the pool as watertight as she could.

For the next two hours she searched for exact rocks, then fit them into place, building up the right side of the pool from one large boulder to another. The three-paces long wall of piling and fitting rock took her four hours total to just get it waist high.

She packed dirt and sand between the rocks where she could, hoping it would work as a form of mortar.

She broke for lunch and went back to work, managing the slightly shorter wall on the left of the pool in three hours.

With that, she staggered back to her camp and made herself the other trout for dinner, made sure Constance was fed and comfortable, then crawled completely exhausted into her bag in her tent before the sun had even left the tops of the mountains.

The next morning, at sunrise, she could barely move. She could feel muscles she didn't even know she had. But a few cups of hot tea and some fried bacon got her enough energy to go back to work on the pool.

When she saw it in the early morning light, she was surprised at how much she really had gotten done the day before.

She spent the first hour moving more rocks to support the two tight walls she had built on both sides of the hot water stream. She wanted to make them thicker and again packed hard clay and sand between the rocks and in any gap she could see.

Then she found the rocks she would need to start damning up the water along a two-foot gap between two boulders where the stream flowed downward.

She put rock after rock in there, using smaller rocks to stop any large leaks.

Then, as the water backed up and started to form the pool, she watched and plugged any leaks in the walls she had built, making sure they were very solid and thick.

At first the water was dirty and muddy looking, but she could see that the flow would clear it quickly.

At lunch she took a break, then with a towel, she went back up to the pool.

It was a thing of beauty.

She almost gasped. The pool had filled completely with blue water. The stream was running over the rocks of the dam.

She tested the temperature.

Perfect, just perfect. Not too hot, but not cool either.

There were small leaks in both of her walls and she took off her blouse and worked to stop the leaks from inside the pool and make the walls on both sides even stronger.

Then she built herself a few flat-rock steps to climb into the pool and took off all her clothes. With another flat rock, she climbed in and placed the rock on the bottom of the pool so she would have a place to sit and lean back and relax.

She had been wrong. She had thought this valley to be heaven when she saw it the first time.

Now, with this hot water pool, it really was heaven.

SIX

June 30th, 1902
Hot Springs Meadow, Central Idaho

FLAG ALLOWED herself a long drink of water, then studied her maps. It was one thing to have a topological map and an aerial photo of the valley, it was another to find the place from the ground a hundred years or more before the photo was taken and the map drawn.

Monumental Creek ran beside the trail that led up the canyon to the boomtown of Roosevelt. This trail was getting lots of travel from miners heading in to get rich, but not as much as the trails into Roosevelt from the Middle Fork of the Salmon or the trail over Monumental Summit from Yellow Pine.

Duster was seldom wrong about anything in the past, especially when it concerned this area. But she just knew that

Hot Springs Meadow existed and she was going to find it.

And then Duster was going to buy her a steak.

She was about ten miles below where the boomtown of Roosevelt was in the process of being built when she finally found what she thought was the right small stream leading away from the valley and up a very narrow canyon.

"Think we can make it up that?" she asked her trusty black and white mare Billie Sue, patting her neck. Then with a look around to see if anyone saw where they were going, Flag left the trail and went into the trees and up the stream.

The high-mountain air was hot and dry and she was drinking water faster than she normally did. This was the third small creek she had explored in three days now. The going was slow and rough and a number of times she had left Billie Sue tied up to go on up the stream on foot.

So far, no luck.

But this stream seemed to fit her map and was about in the right place. This one felt right.

Towering over her on both sides were mountains so steep and tall, she couldn't even begin to guess how far up the peaks were, let alone even try to climb them. Those mountains only let the sun into the bottom of the valleys for a few hours every day, but that was long enough to heat up the air, making everything smell of hot pine.

At least this high in the mountains the evenings cooled down quickly.

The sounds of the small creek bubbling over rocks and through fallen trees was the only sound in the narrow valley. The fact that the creek was flowing as much as it was encouraged her.

But the water hadn't felt even slightly warm, which didn't mean anything. If there was a hot springs in a high-mountain meadow ahead of her, it might not drain into this creek.

Sometimes now, after the hundreds of years in the past, she amazed herself at what she would do. At times she could almost no longer remember what she was like before Bonnie and Duster had showed her the caverns under the institute.

But her passion for history and the impact the geology had on the settlers hadn't changed in the slightest. In fact, she had spent ten different trips back just observing the mudslide that came down and blocked Monumental Creek in the spring of 1909 and turned the town of Roosevelt into a mountain lake.

She still wasn't convinced either way as to the cause of that massive mudslide, either the miners working nearby or just a natural occurrence.

Either way, the impact of the geological event was felt through much of the West, destroying a town that had held over ten thousand people in its prime. Many such geological events had impacted the pioneers. And that was what she loved to study.

And live inside of.

Around her the valley walls got so tight, she dismounted and led Billie Sue into the creek so that they could make their way up through the rock cliffs on both sides. During high spring runoff, it was clear from the water marks on the rocks above her, this area was twenty feet deep.

The cold water on her feet actually felt good and she stopped and let Billie Sue drink for a moment while she did as well. Then she kept going, slowly moving up the stream, being very careful with each step. A broken ankle here would lead to a long and slow and painful ride out and back to the institute.

The entire thing felt like she was climbing a never-ending staircase inside of a narrow hallway. She was thankful she didn't have any sort of claustrophobia because the tall rock cliffs above her made this almost feel like a tunnel, especially with all the brush and pine trees.

The walls seemed to close in even tighter if that was possible for almost fifty paces, then it suddenly just opened up again into a flat area that clearly flooded during spring runoff.

She led Billie Sue out of the stream and then mounted up again, moving slowly along the edge of the creek and into a large stand of pine.

And then, on the other side of the stand of trees, the valley opened wide and round and seemingly flat.

And there was a lush meadow in the center of it with the stream winding through it.

The mountains seemed to form a ring around this meadow.

"We found it!" Flag said softly, not believing what she was seeing.

Stunningly beautiful didn't begin to describe the meadow. Greens and yellows of the summer high-mountain grasses filled the meadow. Pine trees and brown rocks surrounded it.

It looked, at first glance, to be larger than a normal football stadium, with the meadow being the playing field in the center.

"Looks to me that Duster is going to owe me a steak," Flag said to Billie Sue, patting her gently. "Now to find the hot springs."

It was then, as she scanned the tree line, that she saw the horse grazing. And then she spotted the camp.

"Someone has beat us to this place it seems," Flag said, her stomach twisting as she pulled out her saddle rifle and cocked a shell into the chamber.

She had run into more trouble with men in college than she ever had here in the old west. But it never hurt to be careful. Especially this far from any hint of civilization.

She put the rifle back in the sheath and moved carefully across the meadow toward the camp.

It didn't seem to be occupied at the moment.

She tied Billie Sue close to the other horse and with her hand on her rifle, she shouted, "Hello? Anyone around?"

"Up the hill behind the camp," a woman's voice came back strong, echoing off the hills.

Flag just shook her head. Finding someone in this narrow, unknown meadow was surprising. Having it be another woman was downright shocking.

Flag took out her rifle and moved slowly through the camp. It looked like the woman had been here for a few days. And that there was only one person, which helped Flag relax a little more.

She went back and put her rifle back on Billie Sue.

There was a slight trail through the trees up the hill toward the cliff face. After about twenty steps Flag could smell the light sulfur smell of a hot springs.

Duster owed her a steak.

So she had found it. No doubt at all.

As she climbed up the hill, a woman's voice asked clearly, "You alone?"

"I am," Flag said.

"Oh, good," the woman's voice said, laughing. "Because I left most of my clothes down in the camp."

At that a blonde woman about Flag's age of late-twenties stood up behind a pile of rocks, smiling. From what Flag could tell, she was naked and the most beautiful woman Flag had seen in a very, very long time.

The woman had short blonde hair, tan skin that contrasted with the blonde hair, and bright blue eyes. She also had wide shoulders that looked like she had been a swimmer at one point.

The woman pointed to the right. "Got to go around that way."

Flag climbed up through the rocks, following a slightly worn trail until she found herself facing a naked woman sitting in a pool of hot water. The woman seemed perfectly at ease with being naked, not something a woman of this time normally was.

And the pool looked like it had been built recently and honestly Flag couldn't imagine the work this woman had done to build it.

"I'm Jenny Linde," the woman said, waving, the smile never leaving her face.

Flag stopped just beside the pool and sat down on a rock, trying not to stare. She had always been attracted to women more than men, but never had she felt this kind of instant attraction before.

And on top of this, the woman's name felt familiar.

More than likely the attraction was from being alone for so many years. Or maybe because this woman was just a knockout in any time period.

"I'm Kathryn Sinclair, but most everyone calls me Flag for reasons long since forgotten in my childhood."

The woman's smile changed to a puzzled look. "You from the institute?"

Flag was sure her mouth opened, but she couldn't say anything.

"I'm from 2021 originally," Jenny said. "I've heard your name around there at times, but had yet to meet you."

"2018," Flag said.

And then she remembered where she had seen Jenny's name before.

"You wrote an article or two about this place didn't you? In a local newspaper out of Cascade. Those articles were how I found this."

Jenny shook her head. "Not yet, I haven't. But it wouldn't surprise me that I do at some point."

"What's your area of study?" Flag asked. "I'm geological impacts on the pioneers and miners."

"Newspapers of the west," she said, smiling. "I've worked at numbers of them over my trips back here."

Flag just nodded, looking at the pool. "You built the rocks to hold the water?"

"I did," Jenny said. "Took me a while and some bruises, let me tell you."

"I'll bet," Flag said. "Mind if I join you? Long days on the trail searching for this place."

"Please," Jenny said. "The water just happens to be warm, but not so hot as to force a person out of it regularly."

"Perfect," Flag said, starting to undress.

"That it is," Jenny said as she watched.

SEVEN

June 30th, 1902
Hot Springs Meadow, Central Idaho

JENNY HAD BEEN so shocked and surprised when a voice called out, she almost couldn't breathe. Thankfully, it was a woman's voice because she had only brought her towel up to the pool. No gun, nothing.

So she had forced herself to answer.

She had just never expected anyone else to find this place, so she had let her guard down. That kind of stupidity could have gotten her killed.

Or much, much worse.

And even more thankfully, when Jenny asked if the woman was alone, she was. So she forced herself to take some deep breaths and relax as the stranger climbed up toward the pool.

Then when she came around the rock, Jenny lost her breath again. The woman was stunning, not in a model-beautiful way, but in her eyes, shape, and intelligence.

She looked almost like a doll, with short brown hair, a round face, and wide green eyes. And it was those eyes that held Jenny.

And then when the woman took her clothes off, Jenny just stared. Jenny's relationships through college had always been women.

Flag was the most alluring of them all. She was clearly an adult woman, but so short she looked like a perfect doll.

Wow, just wow.

And Jenny could tell that Flag was nervous getting into the hot pool, but once they got the introductions done and both of them let the hot water relax them, the conversation became something Jenny realized she had missed and hadn't even known it.

Conversation with a friend.

For the next two hours, they sat naked in the small hot springs and talked and laughed, their voices echoing over the valley. And they talked about everything, from their first times in the past to what their area of study was.

They talked of experiences while back in the past. Jenny was shocked that Flag had died twice. Jenny had managed, so far to avoid that and Flag told her to continue to do so.

Flag was from 2018, and had traveled almost 700 years in the past in five months. Jenny, so far, was just above 300 years in the past in numbers of shorter trips.

So they talked about how their memories of pre-travel were fading slowly as they piled on more and more years. Flag figured that in three years of 2018 time, at the rate she was traveling and doing research, she would be a couple thousand years old.

The idea of that stunned Jenny.

The two of them just kept talking and Jenny loved every minute of it.

After two hours or so, they both realized they needed to get back down to camp before it got too dark and get some food cooking. The sun was just starting to crawl down the canyon wall toward them.

They both made the trek naked, Jenny carrying a towel, Flag her clothes. It was almost more than Jenny could handle it was so erotic watching Flag make her way carefully down through the rocks with only her boots on.

While Flag worked on getting her horse settled in for the night and brushed, and her tent set up close to Jenny's, Jenny went down to the stream and caught them two more trout for dinner.

Then over dinner of fresh trout and some potatoes Flag had brought with her, they laughed and talked into the night, ending with some wonderful hot chocolate that Flag had brought.

By the time they called it a night, Jenny felt she had found a friend.

And she hoped even more at some point, but she sure wasn't going to push it.

EIGHT

July 5th, 1902
Hot Springs Meadow, Central Idaho

FOR THE NEXT WEEK, the two of them talked and ate and sat in the hot springs enjoying the perfect summer days in the high mountains. It was as if Flag had died and found a slice of heaven.

She was sure of it, actually. Wonderful conversation and fresh trout most nights for dinner just seemed to top everything.

They had become very close and had flirted, but it had gone no farther than that.

At least so far.

Flag just wasn't sure how Jenny felt about women other than as friends and Flag didn't want to take a chance on losing the friendship. And she hadn't really asked her directly yet.

And Jenny hadn't asked Flag. Seemed that for both of them they had avoided the topic. And considering how many things they had talked about, that was amazing.

Flag knew for certain that Jenny wasn't in a relationship anywhere, in any time, and she made sure Jenny knew she wasn't either.

It just wasn't often Flag had made friends since college. Not even on the longer times into the past. Something about knowing that the person was already long dead in her time just kept her from allowing herself to get too close.

Of course, in all the trips into the past, she had had some affairs, almost all with women. But for the most part, Jenny was the first she was really letting herself get close to.

And they had talked some about the fact that when Flag started to travel into the past, it was still two years before Jenny would arrive as a researcher. Jenny found it amazing she hadn't seen Flag around the library at all. Jenny would have noticed.

Finally, they both decided that it was time to move on, leave their little slice of heaven and go back into the real world, or at least the real world they had come from the future to study.

On the morning of July 5th, they left the meadow, leading their horses down the steep creek bed to Monumental Creek and then up toward the now-growing town of Roosevelt.

Jenny wanted to get in on the ground floor of the newspaper that would be starting up there next week and Flag had planned on doing measurements of some geological formations in what would become the mining town of Stibnite on the other side of where the Monumental Lodge was being built.

From there Flag had decided she would head over to the town site of Edwardsburg, staying there until late summer. But she promised Jenny when they parted in Roosevelt that Flag would come back through this way before the snow flew, just to say hi and see how it went.

And if Jenny decided to not winter over in the mountains, they could ride back to the Institute together.

Jenny had said she loved that idea.

Flag was stunned at how devastated she felt the moment she rode away from Jenny. Once, a little distance down the trail, she turned back and Jenny was just staring at her, not smiling either.

Clearly the last week had been very important to both of them. But they both had research to do. But the one thing they always had because of being from the Institute was time.

If Jenny felt the same as Flag felt in a few months, then they could take the friendship to a relationship. Or at least deal with the attraction and save the friendship, one way or another.

Flag wanted it to be a relationship, but with Jenny, if she had to, she would settle for the friendship.

The rest of the summer went slowly for Flag. She thought of Jenny all the time. It was the first week of September before she finally made it back to Roosevelt.

The snow would block all the accesses to the new town in just a few weeks. Flag had no desire to get caught in a winter here. She wanted out of the extreme cold and back into civilization and the Institute where she could read and do research.

And if she stayed in the past, she could at least get breakfast down at the Idanha Hotel. Best breads in all of time as far as Flag was concerned.

When Flag ducked her head inside the large tent that served as the newspaper office, she was surprised to only see one man, a guy with a vest and tie, sitting at an old typewriter behind what looked like a folding table.

"Can I help you?" he asked, staring at Flag.

"Looking for Jenny Linde," Flag said.

The man's face turned sour and he shook his head. "I'm sorry. She was working on a story over on Marble Creek about the new trail there. She had an accident. Her horse slipped and she went over and hit her head and died. I'm so sorry."

Flag just nodded to the man and turned and left. Nothing else to say to him.

"Wait!" he said, standing and coming after her.

The guy in the vest came out of the tent and stood facing Flag on the dusty street that stretched down the middle of the growing town. The place smelled of horse manure and the sounds of construction echoed from seemingly everywhere.

"Are you Flag?"

Flag just nodded, still shocked at Jenny's death. And what that meant. They had not talked at all about figuring out a way to get past the years between them back in 2018 and 2021.

Now those years loomed as an impossible wall.

"Jenny's sister came to pick up her things," the man said, "and she wanted me to give you this note."

It was a folded piece of paper. The man handed it to her, said he was so sorry, and ducked back inside the tent.

Jenny couldn't have a sister here, since Jenny was here through the Institute. That wasn't possible, so that must have been Jenny coming back in disguise.

Flag didn't trust herself to open the note in the middle of the street. She had been so looking forward to seeing Jenny again, her wonderful smile, everything. And to have her back in 2021 now seemed impossible.

When Flag returned, Jenny would be still getting her doctorate and three years away from knowing about the cavern.

Flag had lived seven hundred years in the last five months of that time.

She had no idea what to do.

She tucked the note in her jeans pocket and got provisions in the small general store, enough to get her back to Boise, and headed out.

She knew that Jenny wasn't really dead. She had just gone back to 2021 having had just over two minutes elapse.

But now Flag honestly had no idea how she was ever going to meet Jenny again. They were a very long three years apart in real time. And she really had no idea if Jenny was even interested in making an effort to see Flag again.

They had become close, sure, of that there was no doubt. But how close was the question.

The most important question, actually.

It had only been a week.

Flag got headed down the creek and just past where a new cemetery was starting. She almost stopped to see if there was a grave there for Jenny, but that made no sense at all. Jenny wasn't dead in reality, just in this timeline.

Finally, after about a mile of riding along, just trying to keep her emotions in check, Flag stopped.

Sitting in the saddle in the sun above the bubbling sounds of Monumental Creek, she took out Jenny's note and read it.

"The hot springs will be wonderful in the fall."

That was all it said.

And with that Flag started laughing, tucked the note back into her pocket and then, as fast as she could, she headed down the trail to where the small side creek headed off up the hill to Warm Springs Meadow.

The hot springs would be wonderful this time of the year.

Thunder Mountain Series Available...
These novels are available in electronic format or print at your favorite booksellers.

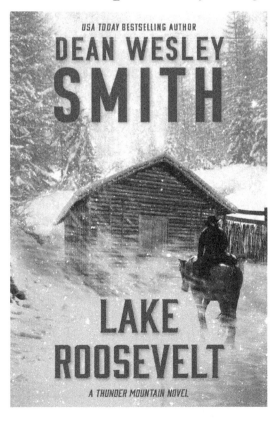

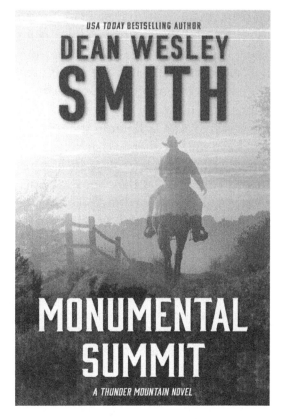

Of that, she had no doubt.

If Jenny was there.

NINE

October 6th, 2021
Boise, Idaho

JENNY FOUND herself back in the small tunnel-like cavern room filled with glowing quartz crystals along both walls. She was three levels under the Victorian house that was the main Institute headquarters in Boise.

She stood in front of one of many small wooden tables in the center of the tunnel, feeling shocked.

Around her thousands of quartz crystals lined the long, narrow tunnel behind wire fence, all in niches, pink glowing gemstones against the gray rock. From what she understood, the quartz crystals all represented a timeline so close to hers as to be indistinguishable. And Jenny knew there were at least fifty more tunnels just exactly like this one in this area.

And also from what she understood, the crystals had been brought here when the Institute was built from a cavern so large and full of them, it stretched into infinity. That was way beyond her history and newspaper brain, but she trusted Duster and Bonnie and the other mathematicians when they told her.

And the crystals took her into the past, into the timeline inside that crystal.

She stared down at the little wooden box on the table in front of her that controlled what time she went into the past of that timeline and then followed along the two cables to the crystal she had hooked to on the wall.

Flag was in that crystal.

Jenny stepped back from the box, then using a glove as she had been trained, unhooked one cord from the box, but left the second cord hooked up and the two cords hooked up to the crystal. She then carefully noted the exact time and date that she had died in the past in that timeline.

The last thing she remembered, she and Constance were working their way up a new trail to get the story on the men building the trail, when a part of the new trail just gave way.

Constance fought to stay on her feet, but the sudden slip had launched Jenny off of Constance.

Jenny remembered the tumble down the slope and the pain until she smashed into a pile of large rocks about twenty feet down the hill and everything went black.

The impact must have killed her almost instantly, because that was the last thing she remembered before finding herself standing here, back in the cavern in 2021.

Now what in the world was she going to do?

She hadn't been able to get Flag out of her mind for the entire month after Flag left. She really, really wanted them to take their friendship to a relationship, but now she had no idea how.

She knew upstairs, somewhere, Flag was here, in this time. But by now she most likely had forgotten all about Jenny. Flag had traveled over 700 years in five months. No telling how many centuries she would have lived now in the last three years.

Jenny let her nerves get the best of her and she just leaned on the wooden table and cried, both from the shock of suddenly dying and also from losing Flag.

Normally she wasn't the crying type. So finally after a few seconds she managed to pull herself back together. She went into the supply room and then up into the large cavern called the Living Room. A small fire was burning in the stone fireplace and there was no one around.

No sign of Flag waiting for her.

Jenny made herself a bowl of soup, then went into the locker room and took a shower and changed clothes, trying to get her mind beyond just dying to figure out what to do next.

She finished the soup while sitting alone at the long kitchen counter and then ate a piece of fresh bread and some peanut butter that had been left.

She realized she couldn't make any decision on her own about this three-year problem.

She had to talk with Flag, find out if there really was a chance of a relationship between them.

And she knew exactly where Flag was and where she was going to be in 1902.

And that was all Jenny needed.

It wasn't much of a plan, but she had no doubt that it was the only hope of answering the question about her and Flag having more than just a friendship.

She had to go back.

She couldn't go back before the moment she died, but she could after. No matter what it took, she had to go back.

Even though in that timeline, in that crystal, she had already died.

Once.

TEN

September 7th, 1902
Hot Springs Meadow, Central Idaho

JENNY had made her way along the trail from Roosevelt after leaving the note

for Flag. She hoped Flag would see it, or if not see it, at least come back to the meadow on the way back to the Institute.

Jenny figured it was their only real hope. Because if they both got back to their present times in 2018 and 2021, meeting again would be next to impossible.

Jenny was still in the last year of her doctorate in 2018. And by 2021, Flag might have lived a thousand years more and barely remember Jenny. More than likely by then she would have met someone, or a hundred someones.

When Jenny got to Roosevelt again, posing as a sister, she had been relieved to hear that Constance had survived and was fine. Jenny would use the horse she had brought from the Institute as a packhorse and would use Constance to ride.

She then picked up her things from the general store where they were being held, including her old slide rule that was really a modern instrument. Then she bought enough supplies for two full months in the meadow.

It had been August 10th that Jenny's sister had arrived in Roosevelt with a black wig, a little too much makeup, and dressed like someone who had a lot of money. No one questioned her at all, since they all knew Jenny had died and she clearly looked like she could be a sister.

Jenny had decided she would wait for Flag until September 20th, two days before the first storm was due to hit and close off the valley. She would need to leave by then.

It took a lot of work to get both Constance and the packhorse up that steep canyon to get to the meadow, but the fact that she knew where she was going helped a lot.

At her campsite, she got the supplies unloaded and both horses taken care of before pitching her tent and starting a fire for dinner.

Then she tucked the black wig into her saddlebag and with her rifle and towel, walked up to the pool where she could wash the makeup off her face and relax.

On the second day, she spent a large part of the day in the pool, making notes in her journal for her book. She had learned a lot about the newspaper in the short month she had worked there before being killed. She needed to get that down before she forgot it.

After that, the days went by slowly. She tried to focus on her work, but most of the time her thoughts just drifted to Flag. And how much she wanted this to work out between them.

She alternated catching trout for meals and using the food she had packed up from Roosevelt.

Every day was sunny and warm, but getting shorter and the nights were clearly getting cooler.

Toward the end of August she spent some time actually exploring the small valley, trying to figure out exactly where would be the best place to build a cabin if she ever wanted to do that here in some other timeline.

Her solution turned out to be right where her camp was. And more than likely it would be possible to set up a system of pipes to get at least warm water into the house.

It would be a difficult, at best, place to live for a winter in this small valley. But with warm water and enough food, it would be possible with the right structure. All that was beyond her capabilities at the moment, but it was fun to think about.

On September 7th, in the middle of the afternoon, Jenny was in the pool making notes about a possible future book when she heard a call.

"Anyone here?"

It was Flag!

Jenny's heart damn near burst out of her chest and it took her a second to catch her breath enough to call out.

"Up in the pool! You alone?"

"I am," Flag shouted back, her wonderful voice echoing off the rocks. "How about you?"

"Alone and naked," Jenny said, then laughed.

Jenny climbed out of the pool and started down the trail, completely naked.

Flag was coming up the trail, smiling the widest smile Jenny could imagine.

In a moment they were in each other's arms, and after that, they were kissing.

And after they both came up for air, all Jenny could say was, "I missed you so much."

"I missed you as well," Flag said, tears in her eyes.

And then Flag kissed her again and it was the most magical moment Jenny could ever remember.

PART TWO
Same Time Next Year

ELEVEN

September 18th, 1902
Hot Springs Meadow, Central Idaho

FLAG KNEW they had to get out of their magical hidden valley with its wonderful hot springs. The last eleven days had been fantastic. They talked and laughed and made love, sleeping in one tent curled up together.

After the fifth night Jenny had said, "Does it feel like we have always slept together?"

Flag had laughed and said, "It feels like I never want to sleep alone again."

Over the eleven days, as the nights got colder and the days never really warmed up much, they talked a lot about what they called "their problem." The three years that separated them in their real time. Besides Flag going back and just waiting for three years for Jenny to return, they could come up with no answers at all.

The crystals they had used to get to this timeline were actually in different parts of the caverns, which as far as Flag understood, they really weren't in the same timeline exactly. But more than likely there was an infinite number of the two of them trying to figure this out in an infinite number of identical timelines.

Past that, Flag had no idea about the math of it all and neither did Jenny.

So they did the next best thing they could think of doing. They decided to stay together right here, in whatever timeline this was, for as long as they could.

So on the morning of the 18th of September, with the sky gray and dark, they headed down the narrow valley to the main trail along Monumental Creek.

From there they had two choices, go up to Roosevelt and over the Monumental Summit and out of the area, or down the stream to Big Creek and then down to the Middle Fork of the Salmon and over to Edwardsburg and out that way.

They had decided to go down, since the trail was easier and less dangerous. So with Flag leading the packhorse and Jenny following on Constance, they worked their way down the trail.

It took them three days of solid riding to reach Boise and the Institute.

They both decided they had a lot of writing and research to do on their books and Jenny had wanted to work for the paper there in Boise, so they settled into one of the wonderful guest rooms in the Institute just as the first snow fell around them in the Treasure Valley.

It was beautiful, as any first snowfall was, and they stood on the large front porch of the Victorian mansion, holding hands, just watching the flakes fall through the large trees. A magical moment that Flag was convinced would be only one of many over the coming years.

A few other travelers were wintering over in Boise and at the Institute, so they had some wonderful meals at times, talking about research and things and events of the past. And on Thanksgiving, both Flag and Jenny cooked a turkey dinner in the Living Room cavern, with all the fixings and a roaring fire in the fireplace. Seven travelers from the future were there, all happy and enjoying the company.

Flag could not believe how much she was falling for Jenny as each month went by.

And Jenny was clearly feeling the same way.

They just fit together.

And for most of the winter, "their problem" never came up.

In late April of 1903, with a great breakfast at the Idanha Hotel to see them off, they headed north toward the mining camps of Northern Idaho. They both had research they wanted to do there.

They stayed up North together, living in a rented house outside of Spokane, Washington, for the next ten years. Both worked on books, shared every detail, and loved every minute of the time together.

After ten years, in the spring of 1913, they returned to Boise and the Institute.

Nothing had changed at all. It felt very strange to Flag how that Institute just seemed to be an island in the stream of time.

With Institute money, they bought themselves a cute little cottage not far from the Institute that looked over the river.

And for the next twenty-three years, they lived there, working, laughing, and loving each other completely.

Then in the summer of 1936, Flag got sick, not with something that even the doctors at the Institute could do anything about.

And they both knew that finally they had to face "their problem."

TWELVE

July 12th, 1936
Boise, Idaho

JENNY KNEW Flag was dying. And she knew that even with the magic of time travel, it might be the last time she would see Flag.

As Flag had gotten sick, they had moved from their wonderful home back into the Institute. Jenny had insisted that if the pain for Flag started to increase, she would help her down into the cavern and pull the wire on the crystal.

Flag would then end up back in November 2018, young and healthy with only just over two minutes having gone by.

And then Jenny would go to the cavern she had left from and pull the wire on her crystal and she would end up back in October 2021 just over two minutes after she left to go pretend to be her own sister.

The years with Flag had been magical. But neither one of them had any idea what would happen next. Flag just couldn't put her life on hold for three years, even though she claimed she could.

And for Jenny, it would be only minutes, no matter what Flag did.

That difference scared both of them a great deal.

Flag claimed she would wait and not travel in time.

But Jenny knew it would never be the same if she did.

They both knew that was the case.

Flag needed to go back and go on with her life and her research and spend the hundreds and hundreds of years in the past, just as she would have planned.

Then, when Jenny returned in 2021, they would talk.

That was all they could figure out to do.

And since the rules of time travel and physics didn't allow them to travel into any time that they were alive, Jenny just couldn't jump back three years.

And they couldn't come back to this timeline, either. Because they had already lived here, time would just kick them into a timeline where they most likely hadn't met yet.

They were stuck with a wall of three years between them.

Finally, the day came that Flag was in such pain, they both decided they had to move.

So Jenny helped Flag down into the caverns and to the room where her crystal was hooked up. Flag had two leather bags over her shoulders full of all her notebooks.

They hugged and kissed, then Jenny stepped back, doing her best to not just cry like a baby.

Flag leaned on the table, clearly in pain, but smiling and crying slightly.

Even forty years older than when they met, Flag was still the most beautiful woman Jenny had ever met.

Or ever would meet.

"Make sure you collect that steak dinner from Duster when you get back," Jenny said.

Flag looked puzzled for a moment, then laughed, which caused her even more pain.

"I love you," Flag said.

"I love you as well," Jenny said.

"See you soon," Flag said, then, with one arm holding her two bags in place, she pulled the wire and vanished.

And for the first time in over forty years, Jenny was alone.

Completely alone.

Flag was gone.

Jenny slumped to the floor of the cave and just sat there crying.

It was all she could do.

THIRTEEN

November 20th, 2018
Boise, Idaho

FLAG UNHOOKED the wire from the wooden box, dropped her two bags of notebooks on the floor, and then slumped to the ground. The pain of her sickness was gone and she was young again. But Jenny was three years in the future.

An impossible three years.

After a few minutes, Flag climbed to her feet and unhooked the crystal from the box that controlled the movement into the crystal and then, as she was supposed to do, marked on the file under the crystal who she was and how long she had been in that past.

Then with her notebooks, she went into the supply area and locker room and changed clothes, leaving her notebooks in her locker there, then headed slowly up the stairs toward the living room. She felt like she was walking in a trance, barely moving her feet. She needed to just get back to her condo and sleep.

Alone.

The thought of that almost made her start to cry, but somehow with a few deep breaths, she held it together.

Duster and Bonnie were still sitting at the counter in the living room talking. Flag has spent over forty years with Jenny in the past, yet here only just over two minutes had passed, plus another ten minutes or so for her to go down to the crystal room and then climb back up.

"Well?" Duster said, glancing around at her.

"There is a hot springs in that valley," she said. "It's wonderful. You owe me a steak. But right now I am so tired, I can hardly move."

"Is everything all right?" Bonnie asked, a look of worry on her face.

"It's been better," Flag said. "I'll explain it to you in a few days, maybe get your help."

Both of them were frowning, but both nodded.

"Just ask," Bonnie said.

"I will," Flag said. "I promise. I'll tell you all about it over that steak dinner."

Duster nodded as Flag turned her back and headed for the stairs to go up and out the back.

A seemingly forever walk later, she opened the door to her condo, stumbled up the stairs to her bed, and cried herself to sleep.

Three days later, on the Friday after Thanksgiving, Bonnie called her to check to see if she was all right. Flag had managed to eat some and just sit on her couch and watch the river go by. The days were gray overcast and fit her mood completely.

She missed Jenny so much, it physically hurt sometimes to even breathe. She had no idea a person could be in such love with another person. But she was. And she needed to fix the problem of her and Jenny no longer being together.

Somehow, on the phone, Flag managed to convince Bonnie she was all right and needed to talk to her and Duster that evening, if she could. Over a steak dinner, maybe.

Bonnie said they would love that after eating so much turkey yesterday and they set a time for six at one of the best steak restaurants in town.

So Flag got her notebook that had all the options on solving "the problem" that she and Jenny had worked on and looked through it again.

Solution one was for Flag to wait. And right now that was what she was planning on doing, writing a lot of books, doing a lot of research, and just waiting the three years until Jenny appeared in the caverns after only being gone for a few minutes her time.

Jenny had been very worried about that solution and how it would make Flag feel. Flag wasn't so worried about it.

The second solution was to talk with Director Parks and allow Flag to jump out of this timeline a hundred years into the future and then just come back three years later, right before Jenny came back from the past.

Neither Flag nor Jenny knew if that was possible. Both thought it might be and would be the best solution if it was possible.

Third solution was for Flag to just go on with her life and research and they would talk when Jenny appeared. But if Flag did that, maybe a thousand years might pass for her and both of them had known Flag would be a completely different person if she did that.

They could come up with no fourth solution.

So that was why Flag needed to talk with Bonnie and Duster. They knew more about time travel into alternate timelines than anyone. They had discovered the original cave of crystals and built the wooden boxes that controlled where a traveler could go into the past.

And with Director Parks' help, they had built the Institute to last through hundreds and hundreds of years. Flag had no idea how far into the future the Institute went.

So if anyone could solve "the problem" it was the two of them.

Flag just hoped there was a solution. Otherwise, she was just going to wait.

FOURTEEN

October 6th, 2021
Boise, Idaho

JENNY APPEARED in the crystal room, touching the wooden box that had sent her back to pretend to be her sister and then live all those wonderful years with Flag.

The room was empty.

That was not at all what she had expected. One way or another, she had expected Flag to be here.

Jenny went about the duties of unhooking the box from the crystal and then labeling the crystal as to where she went and how long she was in that timeline.

Then she went out to the supply area and the locker rooms and changed clothes. Modern jeans, blouse and tennis shoes felt odd after all the years in the past.

She brushed out her hair and washed her face. More than likely Flag and others would be waiting for her upstairs in the living room.

But when she arrived there, no one was around. A small fire was burning in the fireplace, but other than that no sign of anyone.

She couldn't believe this was happening. Something horrid must have happened to Flag.

Or Flag went on to live a thousand years in the past and had forgotten about her. Jenny didn't want to think about that. Not the way she was feeling at the moment.

She got herself a bottle of water from the fridge behind the counter, then went to the elevator and went up to see if Director Parks was in his office. He wasn't.

The entire mansion felt empty.

So Jenny went out through the back door and walked down the river path toward her condo, hoping beyond any reason that Flag would be waiting there.

The condo was empty. The dishes Jenny had left that morning before heading to the Institute were still in the sink. She had lived over forty years in the past with Flag, had died once, and almost no time had passed here.

"Flag?" Jenny said into the quiet of her condo. "Where are you? What happened?"

She had no answers at all.

Not one.

FIFTEEN

November 23rd, 2018
Boise, Idaho

FLAG USED an Uber to get to the restaurant, a place called Steven's. She had only been in the place once before, mostly because it felt far, far too expensive for her, even though she had more than enough money now.

Duster and Bonnie had just arrived and were being shown to their booth when Flag entered. The smell of steak seemed almost too thick to walk through, and Flag realized at that moment just how hungry she was.

The place was built from dark-stained massive old lumber and the booths were large and almost private in nature, with old barn wood walls between the booths.

And plants, lots of plants, everywhere. Flag had no idea how the plants survived in the thick smell of cooking meat, but somehow they did.

The person who showed them to the booth was a nice man Duster's height with a large smile and no hair. He got them settled and took their drink order and when he turned away, Bonnie reached over and touched Flag's hand.

"Are you all right?"

Flag had decided she was just going to blurt it out, so she did.

"Nope," Flag said, shaking her head. "Fell in love on that trip with a wonderful woman named Jenny Linde. She is a traveler as well from 2021 and we spent over forty years together before I got sick and we had to come back."

"She originally wrote the article in that newspaper that got you looking for the hot springs?" Duster asked.

"She did," Flag said, nodding. "And she had built a wonderful rock pool in the small valley by the time I got there."

Flag looked at Bonnie, who was frowning.

Duster didn't seem to notice. "So you are now worried about how to cross the three year gap and be together, right? Be there when she returns?"

Flag again nodded, feeling slightly relieved. "Neither of us knew the mechanics of the alternate timelines and if that was even possible without me just waiting the three years until she arrived. Something I plan on doing if nothing else can be worked out."

"That serious, huh?" Duster asked, smiling.

"Very much so," Flag said. "My first in over seven hundred years now."

But Bonnie wasn't smiling. She took out her phone and quickly dialed a number. "We need you to join us with your computer. We need information on a future traveler named Jenny Linde."

Bonnie listened for a moment, then nodded and hung up.

"The director was on his way home," Bonnie said, "so he will swing by here in a few minutes."

"What's wrong?" Flag asked.

"Maybe nothing," Bonnie said, "but I want to make sure the director is here before we decide what to do."

At that moment the drinks came and Flag quickly realized there was a third place in town that did perfect Margaritas.

"So tell us about this Hot Springs Meadow?" Duster asked.

For the next ten minutes, Flag described the place and how fantastic it was.

"Wow, I wish I would have known that it was there a few thousand years ago," Bonnie said.

"How did she find it?" Duster asked.

"Director Parks allowed her to take an instrument disguised as an old slide rule that tested for sulfur in water."

"I did what?" Director Parks asked as he slid into the booth beside Duster.

"Tell him the gist of your story with Jenny Linde," Bonnie said.

So Flag did.

And all the while, Parks just frowned. When she was finished, he nodded and opened up his computer.

It didn't take him long before he turned the computer to face Flag. "Is this the Jenny Linde that you know?"

A smiling image of Jenny filled the computer screen, which just made Flag smile and nod.

Parks turned the computer back and started to work again.

Bonnie put her hand on Flag's again and said, "Why I was puzzled is because the three of us move up and back through the future of the Institute. We never recruited a Jenny Linde I'm afraid."

Flag looked into Bonnie's eyes and knew she was telling the truth.

Parks nodded. "We never got the chance in this timeline. She was killed by a drunk driver seven months ago just after finishing her first doctorate."

He again turned the computer around so that Flag could see the article about the accident.

She felt the room spinning slightly. "How is this possible?"

"Where we live is just another timeline, just like all the ones we visit through the crystals," Duster said. "In this timeline, Jenny was killed. In other timelines, she lived and we recruited her to travel and do research."

Flag sat back, fighting to keep the tears and the blackness from just coming up and swallowing her.

"You loved her that much?" Bonnie asked.

Flag didn't trust herself to talk, so she just nodded.

Parks closed his computer.

Duster said nothing.

What was there to say? Jenny was dead.

Really dead.

SIXTEEN

October 7th, 2021
Boise, Idaho

THE NEXT MORNING, after an almost sleepless night where she woke up to any noise thinking it was Flag coming in, Jenny made an appointment to talk with Director Parks to find out what had happened to Flag over the last three years.

There was a part of Jenny that couldn't believe that Flag would have forgotten her. They had played up October 6th, the day she returned, as the first day of the rest of their lives. Even if Flag had lived thousands of years in the past, hadn't figured out how to bridge the three years, Jenny still believed she would have been there yesterday.

No matter what. And that left only one conclusion.

Something must have happened.

Director Parks, a six-foot-tall handsome man with a warm smile and dark eyes that didn't miss a thing, welcomed her to his office. It was on the second floor of the old Victorian mansion that sat over the caverns and had touches of the old 1880s when the mansion was built as well as modern improvements. The dated drapes on the tall, massive windows were open, letting in the sun from the bright fall day.

The wallpaper looked original to the time the mansion was built, but the desk and his computer were state-of-the-art modern.

His office chair was high-backed and modern while the other chairs in the room looked to be period.

Parks was dressed in jeans, a dress shirt, and no tie. He looked completely comfortable and at ease.

And worried.

Clearly he could sense something was wrong for her.

He indicated she should take a seat in one of the chairs near the window, making sure she was in the warming sun, and he took a seat sort of facing her.

"So what can I help you with, Jenny?"

"I found that hot springs on Monumental Creek I was looking for," she said. She took the slide-rule-like instrument she had been holding and handed it to him.

"Can't begin to tell you how happy that will make Duster and Bonnie," he said, smiling. "What is the place like?"

"A beautiful high meadow about the size of a football stadium," she said. "Wonderful trout in the stream and a perfect place to camp. I made a rock pool that captured the hot water coming down. It was heaven."

"Sounds like it," Director Parks said. "Are you willing to tell the rest of us where it is at?"

He smiled at that and she laughed slightly. "Of course. And that is what I am here about. I met another traveler in the meadow, a woman by the name of Kathryn Sinclair, but she goes by the name of Flag. I had heard her name before and we got along great. In fact, we spent over forty years in the past as a couple. She was from 2018 and was supposed to meet me when I got back yesterday."

Director Park had put on his poker face and he was looking down at the old slide rule in his hands.

"So what happened to her?" Jenny asked, starting to panic.

"We don't know," Parks said.

"What do you mean you don't know?"

"We don't," Parks said. "Over the centuries going forward and since Duster and Bonnie started this, we have lost three travelers. Two of them we are sure they set a time to back to when they were alive, even though we warned them not to. What happens when a traveler does that, or stays past their own birth date in a timeline, they are in essence kicked out. Duster can tell you all the math of that. Mostly beyond me. But we do know they end up in the caverns with an infinite number of crystals and where time does not move like it does here. More than likely both of them died in those caverns."

"But Flag?"

"Let me show you what we know," Director Parks said and stood.

Jenny stood, surprised that her legs would hold her. She followed Director Parks down into the Living Room and then farther down into the rock caverns where the crystals were stored.

He went to the second door out of fifty along the long narrow hall and opened it. He motioned for Jenny to go into the cavern. It looked exactly like all the others she had been in. A long wooden table up the middle of the narrow cavern and thousands and thousands of pink glowing crystals in pockets in the rock walls on both sides. A chain-link fence blocked anyone from accidentally stumbling into a crystal since no one really knew how much power they really contained.

Duster had told her in the first few days of her training about the caverns

that touching a crystal would kill her instantly, he was fairly sure of that. He had also said that no one wanted to test that theory.

On the table were the wooden control boxes and near the back of the long tunnel one box was hooked up to a crystal on the right wall.

Director Parks pointed to the ledger under the crystal where a traveler logged in. It had Flag's name on it.

The box was still hooked up to the crystal.

"It's been like that for around three years," Director Parks said. "We don't know exactly when she went through. Whenever it was, she never came back."

"No one has tried to pull the wire?" Jenny asked.

"Doesn't work that way from this end. The wire needs to be pulled from the other side to return Flag to here."

Jenny just stared at the box and then the crystal the wires were hooked onto. She felt numb, completely numb.

"Duster, Bonnie, and all our best mathematicians are working on this, trying to figure out what happened and where Flag is. But at the moment, we really don't know."

Jenny moved over and looked at the time Flag had set on the box.

"June 17th, 1902. We met in late June that year at the hot springs. She found it because of some articles I wrote about the hot springs in some newspapers a few years later."

"Really?"

Director Parks seemed surprised at that. "Let me see if I can track down Bonnie and Duster. All four of us need to meet. Are you up for that later today?"

"Anything," Jenny said, staring at the box still hooked to the wall. Only two

Now Available
from all your favorite booksellers
in trade paper and electronic editions.
The book that started the Cold Poker Gang.

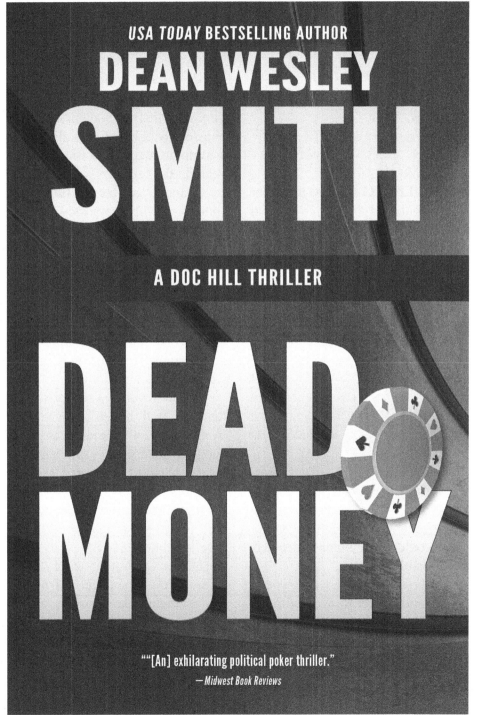

USA TODAY BESTSELLING AUTHOR

DEAN WESLEY SMITH

A DOC HILL THRILLER

DEAD MONEY

""[An] exhilarating political poker thriller."
—*Midwest Book Reviews*

minutes and fifteen seconds were supposed to go by in each trip into the past.

She and Director Parks had been standing here much longer than that.

Flag was in trouble.

And Jenny had no idea what to do about it.

SEVENTEEN

November 23rd, 2018
Boise, Idaho

THAT EVENING Flag went to her office and researched all she could find on Jenny, her education, the accident that killed her.

Everything.

The pictures of her just made Flag cry. But she left them up and even printed a few of them out to put in her home and another to put here in the library office.

There was no doubt that in this timeline, Jenny was gone. The "problem" of the three years that the two of them had worried about for almost forty years just wasn't the problem. The problem was much, much worse.

And Flag needed a lot more information about how traveling back in time to alternate timelines worked. And she needed to understand timelines better before she could even begin to understand any possible solution.

So three days later she got permission from Bonnie and Duster to work with the institute's mathematicians to teach her.

Both Bonnie and Duster agreed, without hesitation.

It took almost a year, and not one day, not one moment of that year, did she stop thinking about and loving Jenny. Flag just

never thought that would be possible in her life, to love one person so completely.

By the fall of 2019, Flag thought she knew enough about the basic workings of alternate timelines and the reason the crystals existed in the first place to start to figure out a few plans.

Plan one was simple.

Basically, she and Jenny had been working under a false premise. They both felt that their original timeline was more important than any other. When in reality, both of them were actually anchored in a completely different timeline a hundred years in the future.

Granted, as far as time itself was concerned, the years they lived in their original timeline were what mattered. Or at least, as far as Flag and the mathematicians like Bonnie and Duster and the others could figure, the original timeline served as an anchor of sorts.

When Director Parks took Flag a hundred years in the future, holding onto him, he made very sure that they then returned a good half hour after they left.

But in a working reality, this timeline that they both hoped to meet and launch from was exactly the same as the one they had spent over forty years together in.

So what Flag wanted to know was why couldn't she go back and find an alternate timeline with Jenny alive and then figure out a way to make that their base timeline.

Duster and the other mathematicians quickly shot that out of the water for mathematical reasons Flag barely understood.

There was only one base timeline for each person and in this one Flag was alive and Jenny was dead.

Plan two was Duster's. "Why not just go back, meet Jenny again at the hot springs, and live another wonderful life in the past, then repeat for as long as you both want."

"But she will still be dead here," Flag had said.

"She will be," Duster said, nodding. "But in a large number of timelines, she is not dead and that is the woman you fell in love with."

"I will have the forty years of memories of us being together," Flag said. "In a new timeline Jenny won't."

Then Duster said something that shocked Flag down to her bones.

"Maybe your Jenny is going back to wait for you there as well. Ever thought of that?"

Flag had not.

But more than likely Jenny and the Flag of her timeline were working things out. Flag had to assume she was alive in Jenny's timeline.

So Flag kept working and learning and then found plan three.

She suggested that if she went back to 1902, found Jenny, and then held onto her and brought her to this present, Jenny would be anchored here, after she had died here.

That idea sent off the mathematicians into a frenzy trying to do the calculations. It seemed that Jenny was clearly alive in other timelines in 2018, those being her base. But since she was dead in this one, would it be possible to bring across another Jenny, from another timeline, to here?

After three weeks, no one computer program or mathematician could answer that question to anyone's satisfaction.

It was possible that Jenny would just be yanked into the caverns.

Or it might work.

Any chance of it killing Jenny, Flag wanted no part of it. So until the math

showed a 100% possibility of success, that idea was off the table.

So just before Christmas of 2019, Flag decided it was time to go see if she could find Jenny again.

So much time had passed that Flag decided to glance at her research that she had done before going back the first time.

But to her shock, she now found new articles written by a Jenny Linde as well as the original ones. But these were written two years after Flag had gotten sick and they had both decided to come back to their original timelines.

Jenny had gone back to try to contact her. Of that there was no doubt.

Before Flag started reading any of the new articles, she did a complete search to make sure she hadn't missed any. There were only three new ones, all short, all seemingly puff pieces about the most remote hot springs in all of the lower forty-eight states.

In all three it said simply, "Discovered in late June of 1902."

Then in all three, Jenny had said as her closing line. "I would love to have lived in those early times, to go back to June of 1902."

That afternoon, Flag showed the articles to Duster and Bonnie.

Both had just laughed.

"Have fun," Duster said, as Flag headed out of the Living Room cavern and back to 1902.

EIGHTEEN

June 20th, 1902
Hot Springs Meadow, Central Idaho

IT HAD BEEN EVERYTHING Flag could do to not rush through any preparations on first getting back to 1902, then with what she packed at the Institute before heading out.

It took three long days to finally get to the Monumental Creek where the small stream from the meadow came down a steep, narrow rock canyon.

Flag's stomach was twisting so bad, she didn't know what to do. She had lived a year thinking Jenny was dead, now she might either find no one in the meadow, or find a new Jenny from different time-lines who didn't know her, or find the Jenny she knew.

Flag made herself go slow and carefully up the stream bed, making sure that each step was solid. Slipping and twisting an ankle or breaking a leg right now would be impossible to deal with.

When she finally mounted back up and headed through the stand of pine trees at the bottom of the meadow, she felt like she wanted to be sick, she was so worried about what she would find.

On the other side of the pines, as with the first time here, the meadow was stunningly beautiful, the grass bright green contrasting against the bright blue sky. The mountains towered around the bowl of a valley like guardians.

And there, on the far side of the meadow, Constance was browsing.

A tent was set up and a camp done.

Flag felt like she was in a trance as she rode across the meadow and up to the camp.

So Jenny was here.

Now the question was which one?

"Anyone home?" Flag managed to shout as she dismounted and let her horse graze beside Constance. Flag's throat was so dry with worry the shout hurt.

"Up above the camp in the rocks," Jenny's voice came back. "Are you alone?"

"I am," Flag said. "Are you?"

"Very much," Jenny's voice came echoing back.

There was a long pause, then Jenny shouted, "Flag is that you?"

"Jenny!"

Somehow Flag managed to run through the camp and started up through the rocks toward the hot springs pool.

"Holy shit!" Flag heard Jenny say, "Is this even possible?"

A moment later a very naked, very beautiful Jenny appeared, crying and smiling at the same time.

Flag had no doubt in the slightest she was doing the same thing.

It took only seconds and they were in each other's arms.

And for Flag, that was how it always should be.

NINETEEN

October 7th, 2021
Boise, Idaho

JENNY MET Bonnie and Duster and Director Parks in his office two hours after she and Parks visited the cavern where Flag had left from all those years before. Three chairs were pulled up in front of Parks' large mahogany desk and Parks sat behind the desk.

Bonnie and Duster were already seated.

The last two hours had been really hard for Jenny. She had decided that even though the day was cold, the sun was out so she needed to walk. She had spent the last two hours just walking along the river path below the Institute, thinking, worrying about Flag, and trying to wrap her mind around what Parks had told her.

"So you met Flag in the past?" Duster asked.

Parks glanced up from his computer and smiled at her. "I told them a little but you might want to fill them in on the entire story."

So Jenny sat beside Bonnie in front of Parks' desk and told the two founders of the Institute how she and Flag had met, what they had done to avoid coming back, and what options they felt they had in dealing with the three years of separation problem.

Bonnie and Duster just sat silently, nodding.

Then when she was done, Bonnie said simply, "Sounds like you and Flag found something very special."

"We did," Jenny said.

"And Flag found you from some articles you wrote about the meadow?" Duster asked.

Jenny nodded.

"So I think you need to write some more articles," Parks said, smiling, "see if we can figure out exactly where Flag is at."

"Or at least warn her," Duster said.

Jenny just felt confused.

Duster and Bonnie both nodded.

"When did you two come back? From what year?"

"1936," Jenny said. "Flag was dying. I watched her vanish from the crystal room, then I went to another crystal room and came back to here as well."

"So 1937 would be safe," Parks said.

Jenny still felt confused.

Bonnie smiled. "We're thinking that if you went back to 1937 and wrote a few more articles about the hot springs, Flag would find them. If you could plant something in the article that Flag would know."

"Like meeting you in 1902 at the hot springs again," Duster said.

"That way," Bonnie says, "If your Flag saw it before she left, and you met her, you would be able to tell her what happened in this timeline."

"And maybe stop it," Parks said.

"You mean change the fact that Flag is missing here?" Jenny asked. "Is that even possible?"

"It is," Duster said. "I could explain the math to you, but trust me, it would be boring."

"So what do I need to do," Jenny said.

"Go back to 1937, write some articles," Bonnie said, "then come back and head to the hot springs in 1902 and hope Flag shows up."

"But it won't be the Flag of this timeline," Jenny said.

"We don't know that," Duster said. "It is clear she was going to 1902 when something happened. We think something happened there, not on the jump there."

"And we feel that Flag is smart enough that if warned, she might be able to avoid this outcome," Parks said.

Jenny nodded to that and then for the next two hours Duster and Bonnie explained to her some of the things she might need to tell Flag while Jenny took careful notes. The last thing she wanted was for her to tell Flag something that was wrong and cause this.

And with traveling into alternate timelines, anything was possible.

TWENTY

June 20th, 1902
Hot Springs Meadow, Central Idaho

JENNY flat couldn't believe when she heard Flag's call that Director Parks' idea had worked.

But somehow, it had.

Now it was up to her to rescue Flag, if that was even possible. She didn't even know for sure what Flag needed to be rescued from exactly.

After the longest and most wonderful hugging and kissing on the trail up to the hot springs pool, and more "I love you" and "I missed you" statements than could be counted, Jenny guided Flag down the trail toward the camp.

It felt so right to have Flag beside her again.

Fantastically, unbelievably right.

In camp, Jenny slipped on a blouse and nothing else and then helped Flag get her horse taken care of. Actually, Jenny knew she hindered more than she helped because she kept wanting to hug Flag.

And Flag kept wanting to hug Jenny, saying over and over that this was impossible and a miracle.

And Flag kept telling Jenny how beautiful she was.

Jenny thought Flag just as beautiful.

"So even though you had to take care of me as an old, dying woman, you still find me beautiful?" Flag asked.

Jenny just laughed. "I found you beautiful when you were old, as beautiful as I find you now."

That delayed taking care of the horse a little longer because Flag just threw herself into Jenny's arms.

Finally, they got Flag settled into camp. It was just past noon and Flag left her clothes on her saddlebag and the two of them climbed naked back to the pool, working their way through the rocks and up the trail hand-in-hand.

All Jenny could think about was how right this felt.

And wow, did they have a lot to talk about.

As they sat holding each other in the crystal-blue warm pool, Jenny could tell Flag was slowly getting worried.

Jenny had a hunch Flag could sense the same thing from her. After all those decades together, they knew each other.

"I got to tell you what happened when I got back to 2018," Flag said, leaning back and staring at the rock walls above them.

Jenny nodded. "And then I will tell you what happened when I got back to 2021."

Flag nodded, then she took a deep breath and told Jenny about talking with Bonnie and Duster at dinner and the three-year problem.

"But when I mentioned your name," Flag said, "They looked puzzled and called Director Parks to join us. He said you had never been a traveler in my timeline."

"I wasn't?" Jenny asked, sitting up and facing Flag directly, feeling completely shocked. How was that even possible?

Flag nodded, clearly upset. "If fact, you died in a car crash just before finishing your first doctorate."

Jenny instantly remembered that rainy night. The drunk driver had come right at her, in her lane, far, far too fast for the two-lane road in the hills near Stanford. For some reason, instead of swerving to the right and deeper into her own side of the road to try to miss him, she had yanked the steering wheel left into the oncoming lane. Later she had told the police her instant thought was that there was room on that side of the road and the hillside and ditch were there instead of the drop on her side down into rocks and a gulley a couple hundred feet below.

The guy had gone right and would have smashed solidly into her if she had tried to stay on her own side of the road. As it was, he clipped her car and went off the road, rolling down into the gulley. She was in the hospital for a few days. He died.

They found out later he was suicidal and was looking to kill himself by car.

Jenny told Flag the entire story. "I have no idea why I went left into his lane to avoid him. If he had come back into that lane, I would have died, but he went more right into my lane instead and I survived."

"In my timeline, and an infinite number of others, you did not," Flag said, her voice only a whisper.

Jenny kissed her, hard and long.

"I am right here," Jenny said when they came up for air. "We are together. That is what counts, isn't it?"

Flag smiled and nodded. "It is."

"So now let me tell you what happened when I got back in 2021," Jenny said.

Flag nodded.

"You weren't waiting for me," Jenny said.

"Oh, shit," Flag said, a shocked look on her beautiful face. "What happened? There is no way I wouldn't have been there waiting for you. Did I die in your timeline?"

Jenny kissed Flag again and smiled. "No, you did not die. And I know that you would have been there, but I kept thinking that you went on with your life, lived a thousand years, and just forgot."

"Never happen," Flag said. "Not after what we shared for all those years. I want a thousand more years like those."

"I believed that," Jenny said, "so I went to talk with Director Parks and he was stunned that I had met and spent time with you."

Flag looked puzzled. "Why would he be stunned at that? What happened? What did I do?"

"Sometime after you returned to 2018, you took another trip here, to 1902. Maybe this trip. We don't know. But you never returned."

"Never returned?" Flag asked, looking very puzzled.

Jenny nodded. "Director Parks showed me the crystal you went through. It was still attached and had been for over three years. Only three people in all the hundreds of years of the institute have not returned. You are one of them."

Flag sat back nodding.

Jenny was surprised that Flag wasn't more upset. So Jenny went on.

"Director Parks and Duster suggested I go back to 1937, after we left the last time, and write a few more articles about this hot springs."

"I found them," Flag said, smiling.

"But I didn't find them in 2018, but instead in 2019, after I had studied alternate timelines and time travel for a year with the mathematicians. So in your timeline, something else happened to that Flag."

Jenny was shocked and impressed. "You spent a year studying the math of timelines?"

Flag nodded. "In my timeline, you were dead. So I had the time. I knew in an infinite number of others, you were still right here and as beautiful as ever. I had to understand at a deep level what would be possible for us and a very long future together."

"Have I ever said how much I love you?" Jenny said, moving over and straddling Flag and kissing her and holding her.

Flag laughed when they came up for air, then said, "I'll never, in a hundred thousand years, get tired of hearing that."

PART THREE
Timeline Confusion

TWENTY-ONE

June 21st, 1902
Hot Springs Meadow, Central Idaho

THE NEXT DAY, before heading back up to the hot water and after a wonderful night together, just holding each other near the fire and staring at the stars, Jenny showed Flag the notes she had a taken from Bonnie and Duster.

They had just finished an easy breakfast and were cleaning up. Around them birds were chirping and the sun had just hit the valley floor promising a warm day ahead.

After a year of study of time travel and alternate timelines, Flag knew most of what was in the notes. Besides living past her own birthday in 1986 which would cause her to be kicked out of the timeline and into the caverns where all energy, matter, and time mixed, she had no idea how she could have done something in this timeline that wouldn't allow her to return.

So more than likely she hadn't. For some reason she had returned, but made it appear to Jenny and others that she hadn't.

Occam's Razor applied. The most likely answer was usually the right answer and the most likely answer was that the being lost in time was a false trail.

And basically Bonnie and Duster had said the same thing in their notes they had given Jenny. The notes didn't seem focused at all on how Flag got stuck, but more on how a traveler can merge timelines. Flag had read some on that topic over the year of her studies, but wasn't entirely certain what they meant. But it was Bonnie and Duster and they wouldn't have told Jenny to tell her to focus on that without a reason.

So Flag would focus on merging timelines.

As Flag and Jenny talked while they finished cleaning up and brushing the horses, Jenny got that wonderful puzzled expression on her face that was one of the many, many thousands of things Flag loved about her. It meant that Jenny's powerful brain was wrestling with something.

Finally, in a long moment of silence, Flag just smiled at Jenny and said, "So what are you trying to figure out?"

"What happens if you did come back to my timeline in 2018 and didn't unhook the cord and sign out of the ledger for some reason? Wouldn't that make everyone think you were stuck in the past somehow?"

Flag nodded. Jenny had figured it out as well.

"I have no idea why you would do that," Jenny said, going on. "And not tell anyone as well."

"I have no idea either," Flag said. "But it seems pretty clear that some timeline versions of me did just that. Did Parks tell you why they hadn't just pulled one wire on the crystal on their end to bring me back?"

"He said it doesn't work that way."

Flag smiled and hugged the love of her life. "It does work that way. They just had a reason to not do that, to not tell you."

"You mean they could have pulled you back into the timeline at any moment?" Jenny asked.

Flag nodded. "If I wasn't in the cavern, absolutely. That machine gets unhooked from either side and any traveler returns from any timeline in 2 minutes and 15 seconds elapsed time. No exceptions unless the traveler is in the caverns where time and space and energy merge."

"So why pretend you had vanished all those years?"

"More than likely," Flag said, smiling, "I asked them to. More than likely it was all a show for you."

"And why would you do that?" Jenny asked, looking very, very puzzled, which just made her even more beautiful if that was possible.

"Because I wanted to spend a few thousands of years with you," Flag said as they walked hand-in-hand from brushing the horses back into their camp.

"I like that idea," Jenny said after the wonderful kiss tapered off. "But I have no idea what you are talking about."

"I honestly need to think it through as well," Flag said. "So how about we do that naked in hot water?"

"Damn," Jenny said, laughing. "I thought you would never ask. And by the way, this higher-math stuff just makes me horny."

And with that she just started stripping off her clothes and all Flag could do was stand and stare and marvel at how lucky she had gotten finding Jenny in all of time.

TWENTY-TWO

June 23rd, 1902
Hot Springs Meadow, Central Idaho

THE SUN was just starting to hit the canyon walls the next morning as Jenny worked to cook them breakfast. Fresh trout they had caught the night before along with coffee and the last of some bread Jenny had brought with her from Boise. Nothing like the smells of fresh trout sizzling in a frying pan and coffee brewing to cut through the chill of the morning air.

Flag was sitting in front of their tent, scratching in her notebook, an intent look covering her face. Jenny almost felt guilty bothering her.

But at that moment Flag stood, put the notebook aside and said, "That smells wonderful and I'm starved."

"Get it figured out?" Jenny asked as she gave Flag a plate of trout and a cup of coffee.

"I think so," Flag said, nodding. "We have to merge a bunch of timelines to really make this work."

Jenny just shook her head and both of them sat on rocks close enough to the fire to let the heat from it keep them warm as they ate. Neither said a word as they started in on the trout.

Finally Jenny said, "So how do two wilderness girls camping by a hot springs go about merging timelines?"

That sounded so stupid, she couldn't believe she had even said it. Of course, traveling into the past and meeting a woman from another timeline in a mountain valley on the surface didn't sound that smart either, but that was what had happened.

Flag laughed, took another bite of trout, then took a stick they used to poke the fire and drew a line in the dirt in front of them.

"That's the timeline we are now in. It's just like an infinite number of others."

Jenny nodded. She understood that much.

Flag drew another line beside the first and parallel to it. "This is the timeline I am from. It is also like an infinite number of others. In it you are killed in college."

Jenny took another bite of trout and nodded, not wanting to think again about that near miss that night.

Flag drew a third line on the other side of the larger line. "That is your timeline where I am pretty sure I just pretended to vanish."

Jenny nodded.

Flag drew a dotted line across all three lines at a ninety-degree angle. "This is the year 2021."

Jenny again nodded as she took another bite of the trout. So far she was following just fine.

"Notice something?" Flag asked. "There are two of me in these timelines in 2021 and only one of you."

Jenny nodded. She had wondered about that for the last two days.

"So," Flag said, smiling and then going back to focus on her trout. "We need to balance this scale. And I have a hunch that is what Bonnie and Duster and the Director are trying to help us do."

Jenny had been following right up to that moment.

"How in the world do we do that?"

"We save your life in college," Flag said. "In that unlimited number of timelines, we stop you from getting killed."

"We can do that?" Jenny asked, stunned at the very idea.

"We can," Flag said, nodding. "With some basic research that I am pretty sure we can do from the Institute in this timeline. And do it together."

"And what is the hope of all of this besides us being together?" Jenny asked, looking at the lines on the ground.

Flag reached out and drew a line from the timeline that Jenny was dead in to the center line. "We divert and merge this timeline into all the others. So you are alive in them all."

They sat for a long, silent moment, letting the morning slowly warm around them as the sun worked its way down the canyon walls toward the camp.

Jenny knew just enough about alternate timelines to know that an infinite number of timelines were formed from every decision. Just as an infinite number of timelines formed on each side of her living or dying.

And she also knew that when a decision made no impact on the future, the timelines melded back together. This happened an infinite number of times every second in every timeline.

But Jenny didn't understand how she and Flag could make that happen.

"So if somehow we figure out a way to save me from being killed in that accident," Jenny said, "wouldn't we create an infinite number of timelines where we didn't save me? So in those I would remain dead?"

Flag nodded. "That's right. But there are ways and the math shows how and actually, from what I vaguely remember in the year of study, Bonnie and Duster have done it a few times. We just have to find the right trigger point where the universes split for that suicidal guy who killed you and blend them there so that he never gets a chance to make the decision that night to kill himself."

"That's the research you are talking about," Jenny said, nodding. She was finally starting to have hope because it was clear Flag had hope.

Flag nodded and smiled.

"One more thing I don't completely understand," Jenny said as she finished her trout and sipped on her coffee. "How

Now Available
from all your favorite booksellers in trade paper and electronic editions.

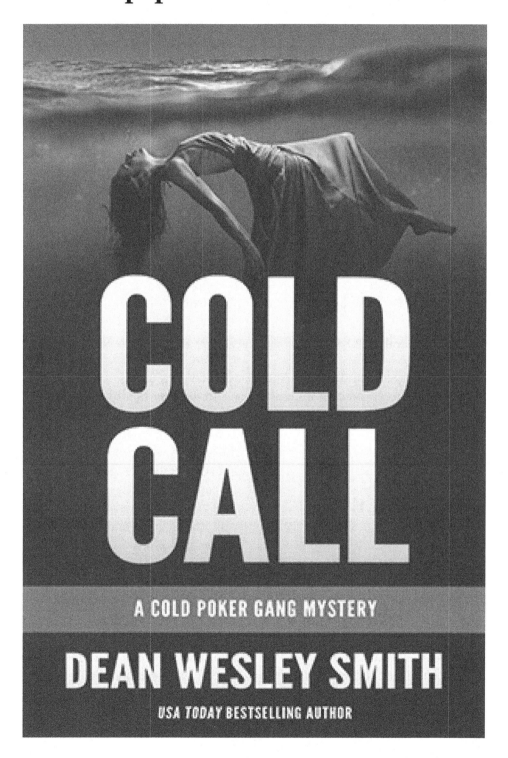

did the Flag of my timeline know about any of this?"

Flag only shrugged. "The Institute exists into the future for hundreds and hundreds of years and it studies and tracks timelines in massive computers I can't even imagine. And Bonnie and Duster and Parks move back and forth through all those hundreds of years."

"So they knew?" Jenny asked.

"Flag shrugged. "More than likely we showed up together at one point in one timeline while we didn't in others and Bonnie and Duster traced it back to us now."

"Did the Flag of my timeline meet another version of me?"

"Maybe, maybe not," Flag said. "But chances are Bonnie and Duster met the me of that timeline at one point and explained it all. They wanted to help you and me."

"That is sort of what they do, isn't it?" Jenny said nodding.

"That," Flag said, nodding. "And more than either of us could ever imagine I would bet."

Jenny could only agree to that.

TWENTY-THREE

July 3rd, 1902
Hot Springs Meadow, Central Idaho

THE WEEK with Jenny in the beautiful high-mountain valley had gone quickly. Flag didn't want it to end, but they had both done everything they could do by just talking and sitting in the hot springs. They both had agreed that they needed to get moving, to see if they could solve their long-term problem.

So as the sun hit the valley floor, bringing the summer heat and smells of dry pine needles to the air, they saddled-up and rode slowly away from their wonderful camp. They had promised each other that if their grand plan to merge timelines didn't work, they would meet back here again no matter what.

They moved slowly, in no real hurry, enjoying each other's company for the three days and nights it took them to reach Boise and the Institute. As normal, except for cleaning, exterior, and stable staff who knew nothing of the caverns below, the big Victorian mansion was empty.

They decided to stay in a guest bedroom on the second floor, enjoying the comfort of the thick feather bed and the wonderful breakfasts at the Idanha Hotel in town every morning.

During the warm afternoons and evenings, they basically camped in the big cavern, talking, doing research, and drinking far more iced tea than should be allowed.

In the year that Flag has spent without Jenny in the future, Flag had done a lot of research on the man who had killed Jenny. His name was James Webber. A very smart and seemingly nice guy who just couldn't get past the sickness of depression.

Flag had traced back his family for a short distance and when Bonnie and Duster told Jenny to think about merging timelines, Flag knew that the answer lay in James Webber's past.

Finally, after two wonderful weeks of research in the institute's extensive paper files of the time, Flag knew they had a plan. But she needed to check it for certain on the computers in her future timeline and with the mathematicians there.

So with Jenny looking worried, Flag kissed her, said, "I'll be back in an hour," and unhooked the wire to the crystal she had come through.

In the future, it took her almost two weeks to confirm all the data they had discovered in the old paper files about James Webber's family. And add a bunch more exact detail about it from family journals.

Then Flag returned to the past and the same exact timeline exactly one hour after she had left.

Jenny had spent the hour Flag had been gone getting a really nice steak dinner ready that almost got ruined because Flag wanted to hug her so much.

So sitting at a table near where in the future the long kitchen counter would be, they ate the juicy steaks with red potatoes and fresh strawberries and real whipped cream for dessert.

And over dinner Flag told Jenny of the weeks of research she had done in the future, what Bonnie and Duster had thought, and what she had found.

"So Webber's great-grandparents meet on a train headed west in about three months?" Jenny asked as Flag finished.

Flag nodded. "That's the key point. She is headed for Portland, he had planned on stopping in Boise, but instead decided to ride on to Portland with her. If we can manage in this infinite number of timelines we are existing in right now to not let that meeting happen, let her go on to Portland alone, the James Webber of the future will not exist. The math says that the meeting was of such a small probability that if we stop the meeting, it will never happen in any timeline. Thus merging all the timelines that split from that point."

"And the Webber family does not have enough impact through time to cause other future timelines to split?"

Flag shook her head. "Surprisingly no. Down the road a few of the Webber descendents besides James cause some timeline splits, but nothing major and not in any fashion that would cause changes in the Institute if they did not exist. In fact, the largest impact to the overall timelines is James Webber killing himself and you in the process. Otherwise the entire family just sort of floats through time doing little to anything of impact."

"Wow," Jenny said. "That's just sad."

Flag could only nod to that.

TWENTY-FOUR

October 18th, 1902
Denver, Colorado

THE SMELL of the trains in the past always surprised Jenny the most. Cigarette and cigar smoke seemed to hang thickly in many of the cars and the constant burning smell coming from the steam engines pulling the trains sometimes left the cars filled with a gray smoke, especially if a few of the windows were open.

Thankfully, due to the cooler days in Colorado in October, the windows of the cars were seldom opened.

The dining car was the exception to the smoke smells since no one was allowed to smoke in there. It usually smelled of fresh bread and brewing tea. Every table was covered in white linen and the silverware always shined. The china plates were so polished you could almost see yourself in them and the food seemingly perfect and tasty. Jenny loved the dining car the most.

She and Flag had taken the forty-one-hour train ride from Boise to Denver and stayed in Denver for a week, making sure they were ready.

The plan was that Jenny was to find Harvey Webber as they got on the train and get his attention while Flag would befriend young Denise Levins who would already be on the train and make sure she stayed away from Harvey.

As they boarded the train early in the morning to head back to Boise, it was not hard to find either of their targets.

Denise was sitting alone against a window, looking very timid and slightly frightened. She had mousy-brown hair pulled up tight in a bun and wore a plain blue dress that showed the wear of her trip from St Louis already. She looked relieved when Flag sat down beside her.

Turned out that young Harvey was no more than twenty, if that, and most desperately wanted to appear older and wiser. Jenny figured the best way to get his attention was to ask him for help with a carpetbag that she had filled with a few books to make it feel even heavier than it needed to be.

He had on a cheap wool suit that more than likely was his best one and carried only one bag. He smiled widely at Jenny's request and seemed to almost trip over himself in trying to help.

Then once their luggage was settled, she sat next to him, something that seemed to please him no end.

Jenny and Flag had both dressed up for the trip, both wearing dresses of the time that showed them to be women of means, yet not too much. Both their targets had little money, which was why they did not have private accommodations on the train. Flag and Jenny had had their own stateroom on the way from Boise.

Jenny was very much going to miss it on this trip.

After an hour into the forty-plus-hour ride as the train worked its way up into the mountains, Jenny had learned that young Harvey hoped to help an uncle in Boise in his new department store. Seemed Harvey had a passion for furniture and from what Jenny could tell, he really knew his passion. Jenny had a hunch that by the time this trip was over, she would know a lot more about furniture of this time period than she had ever wanted to know.

As it turned out, young Harvey enjoyed talking about himself and furniture so much, Jenny had almost no need for the entire trip to use any of her prepared stories.

And from what Jenny could tell from watching four seats ahead of her, Flag and young Denise seldom talked. In fact both just spent their time reading.

Jenny envied that. Flag would owe her for this.

And more than anything, Jenny just wanted to go kiss Flag and hold her. But if this worked, there would be more than enough time for that in the future.

Jenny dined with Harvey, who seemed to not only know furniture, but his manners. He might have talked all the time, but he did treat her with the respect of a woman of the time.

And at night he didn't even snore in the seat beside her, unlike the large man directly behind her who shook the car with his snoring.

And even more amazing, for the entire forty-plus hours, Jenny and Flag managed to not even allow Harvey and Denise to even see each other, let alone notice each other.

Finally, late in the evening of the second full day, the train pulled into Boise.

Jenny watched as Flag said her good-byes to Denise and then waited for Jenny and Harvey to pass her to get off the train.

On the platform of the beautiful Union Pacific Station on the hill overlooking Boise, Jenny gave Harvey her card as a woman of the time might do and said, "I hope we can talk again."

The address on the card was fake, of course, and Jenny had no desire to ever see poor Harvey again, let along hear another story about the carvings on a table leg.

Harvey beamed, shook her hand, bowed slightly, and walked away.

Jenny turned back to the smiling Flag who was coming down the stairs to get off the train.

"Looks like mission accomplished," Jenny said to Flag.

"That it does," Flag said.

At that moment there was a slight shimmering in the air.

And Flag was gone.

Vanished and no one but Jenny had seemed to notice that she had even been there.

And then the next moment the train station vanished and Jenny found herself sitting next to Flag in the large living room cavern of the Institute.

She glanced quickly around. From the looks of the kitchen area, it was 2021 or so.

Bonnie and Duster and Director Parks were sitting on a couch across from her. Bonnie had on a silk blouse and jeans, Duster wore his long coat over a blue shirt and jeans and his cowboy hat sat on the table in front of him, and Director Parks had on a blue silk suit with a light shirt under it and no tie.

All three were smiling.

TWENTY-FIVE

October 19th, 2021
Boise, Idaho

FLAG HAD NO IDEA what the shimmering in the air meant that filled the large cavern under the Institute. It looked like it should be some sort of heat wave, but it had no feeling to it at all.

Across from her on the couch, Bonnie and Duster and Director Parks just smiled and nodded, seemingly very pleased with the strangeness in the air as it passed.

Then the shimmering was gone.

Beside her Jenny laughed, then clapped her hands and said, "We did it!"

Then she hugged Flag harder than she had hugged her when she had arrived back from their first trip earlier in the day and Flag had been waiting for her.

Flag had not one clue what was going on.

After Jenny let Flag go, Duster asked, "Do tell us exactly how it went on the train."

"And realize," Bonnie said, "that this Flag has no idea either what happened. As far as she knows, you just came back from 1934 and your life together."

Jenny turned to Flag, looking worried. "You don't?"

"Not a clue," Flag said.

And she really didn't. Flag had talked with Bonnie and Duster after she had returned from being with Jenny all those years, and they had agreed that the best way to bridge the three years was to just jump into the future and come back to a point in time right before Jenny returned. So that was what Flag had done with Director Parks.

"Oh, my," Jenny said, turning back to face Bonnie and Duster and Director Parks. "I'm not even sure where to begin."

"Start by explaining to Flag that in some timelines," Bonnie said, "you had been killed by a suicidal driver before you came to the Institute."

Flag felt a shock go through her at the very idea that Jenny had died before they met. The Flag in those other timelines must have been devastated to say the least to return to find that Jenny never would be at the Institute.

Slowly, Jenny told the story of how Flag had not been there waiting for her when she returned on October 6th, but that the cover story of her being lost in time had been set up.

That surprised Flag even more. "But I was there this morning."

"Today is October 19th," Bonnie said, leaning forward and smiling, "Not October 6th."

Flag's head was spinning and Jenny just squeezed her hand to help her stay stable.

"Where was I?" Flag asked.

"We sent you a hundred years into the future," Bonnie said.

Flag nodded. "To return to this morning to meet Jenny. So I wouldn't have to wait the three years. I went with Director Parks."

"And I set the time for you to come back for today," Director Parks said, smiling, "the 19th, not the 6th as originally planned."

"How could you have known what was happening in other timelines?" Jenny asked.

"The best way to explain it," Director Parks said, "is that the Institute now extends over six hundred years into the future from this time period. And our computers of that time can handle the massive amount of information needed to track the timelines of our travelers."

"So the three of you talk to your counterparts in other timelines?" Jenny asked.

All three shook their heads. "But we all work from the same information."

Jenny nodded, but Flag was even more confused than ever.

"You said Jenny was dead in many timelines. Is that changed?"

"It is," Duster said, smiling.

Jenny clapped her hands and laughed.

She then went on to tell Flag about how they had gone back again, her from this timeline and Flag from one of the timelines in which Jenny was dead. She then told all of them about what they managed to do on the train, which then changed the fact that Jenny would not be killed by a suicidal driver before finishing college.

"The shimmering?" Flag asked.

"The changed timelines merging," Director Parks said. "It happens continuously, but at such a small scale, we never notice."

"We notice the shimmering when an infinite number of established timelines are merged back," Duster said. "That's what happened when Jenny and Flag kept those two apart on that train."

"We would not have allowed them to do that," Bonnie said, "no matter the results with Jenny in other timelines if the change would have made any real historical difference. In reality, all the timelines created by those two meeting on that train had already merged back together naturally in less than a hundred years."

"So we just sped up the process is all?" Jenny asked.

Duster and Bonnie nodded.

"This is going to take some time to soak in," Flag said.

Jenny squeezed her hand. "Speaking of soaking. You up for a trip back to our hot springs?"

"Together?" Flag asked, smiling.

"Together," Jenny said and leaned over and kissed Flag.

And that felt perfect to Flag.

TWENTY-SIX

June 20th, 1902
Hot Springs Meadow, Central Idaho

THE SUN had already warmed the beautiful round meadow as Jenny and Flag came through the trees and stopped, both just sitting on their horses to enjoy the view.

The smell of hot pine filled the air and the bright green grass on the meadow floor shimmered in a slight breeze. The deep blue of the sky over the brown canyon rocks and high mountains around them just added to the sense that they had just climbed up into heaven.

"Takes my breath away every time I see this wonderful place," Flag said.

Jenny could only nod. It did that for her as well. So many wonderful memories had already happened in this small valley. She had built the hot springs pool twice by herself, but this time Flag would help her and that would make it even better.

That was the way it always should have been. And now always would be.

"I was sort of expecting to see you camped up there," Flag said as they stared across the meadow toward their normal campsite. "Every time I have come to this meadow that has been the case."

"Glad timelines don't work that way," Jenny said, laughing. "I really don't want to share you with another copy of me."

"Now that I agree with," Flag said. "One of you is more than enough for me."

Jenny laughed. "Great answer. You getting hungry?"

"Starving for some of those fresh trout in that stream," Flag said. "I'll set up camp if you do the fishing."

"Deal," Jenny said. "And after that let's build a pool. Together this time."

"I flat love that idea," Flag said.

Side-by-side, the two of them worked their way across the lush, green meadow.

And toward a long future together.

The Year of the Cat Collections

123

COMING NEXT MONTH

All Issues Are All Still Available

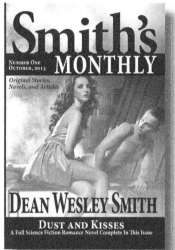

#1...October 2013

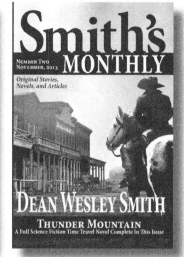

#2...November 2013

#3...December 2013

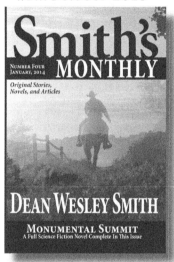

#4...January 2014

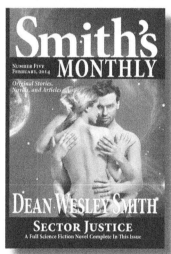

#5...February 2014

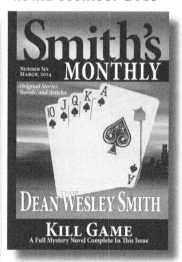

#6...March 2014

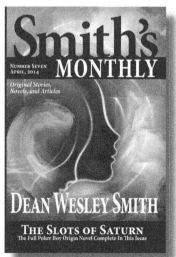

#7...April 2014

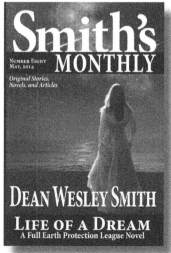

#8...May 2014

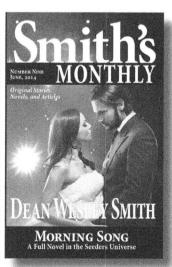

#9...June 2014

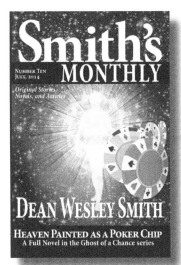

#10...July 2014

#11...August 2014

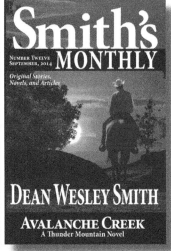

#12...September 2014

#13...October 2014

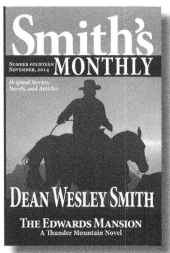

#14...November 2014

#15...December 2014

#16...January 2015

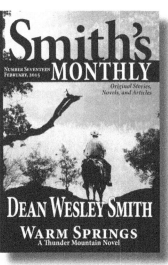

#17...February 2015

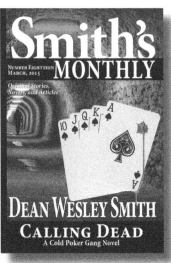

#18...March 2015

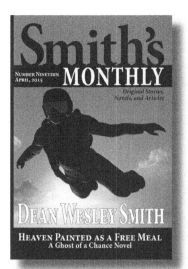

#19...April 2015

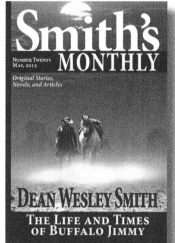

#20...May 2015

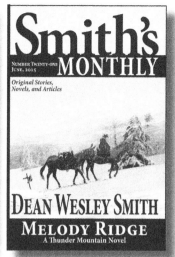

#21...June 2015

#22...July 2015

#23...August 2015

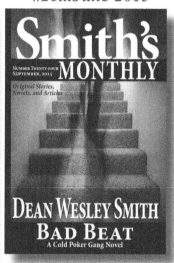

#24...September 2015

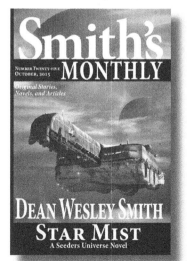

#25...October 2015

#26...November 2015

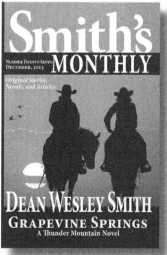

#27...December 2015

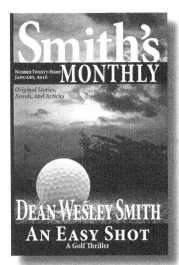

#28...Januaray 2016

#29...February 2016

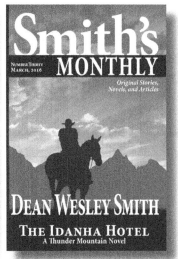

#30...March 2016

#31...April 2016

#32...May 2016

#33...June 2016

#34...July 2016

#35...August 2013

#36...September 2016

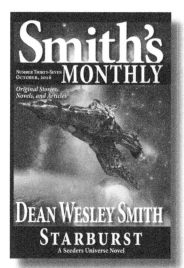

#37...October 2016

#38...November 2016

#39...December 2016

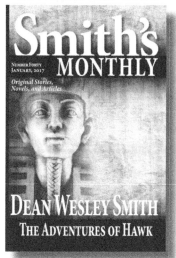

#40...Januaray 2017

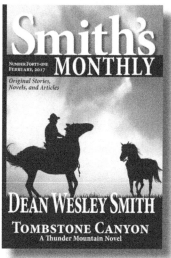

#41...February 2017

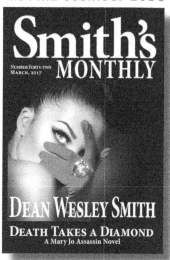

#42...March 2017

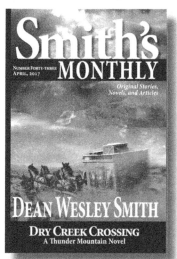

#43...April 2017

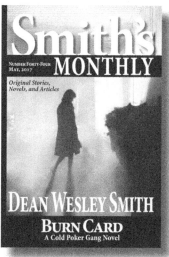

#44...May 2017

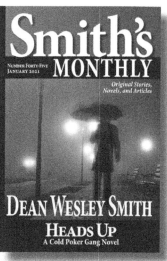

#45...January 2021

Made in the USA
Las Vegas, NV
03 October 2021